BURNING DOWN THE NIGHT

BRYAN SMITH

Grindhouse Press
PO BOX 540
Yellow Springs, Ohio 45387

Grindhouse Press #089
ISBN-13: 978-1-957504-02-5

ONE

April 8, 1994

AT THE START OF THE most momentous day of his life, Cole Watson had no goal in mind other than procuring some extra spending money, so he got some stuff together, hopped in his car, and drove into the city.

Cole's car was a burgundy-colored 1988 Toyota Tercel. Boring but functional, he'd done what he could within his limited means to give it some extra pizzazz. It was adorned with a variety of strategically selected and placed stickers intended to communicate certain important things about himself. In the lower left-hand corner of the rear window was a NIN sticker. He genuinely enjoyed the music of Nine Inch Nails, but the real reason this sticker warranted such prominent placement was something he'd noticed in the years since the 1989 release of *Pretty Hate Machine*.

A really high percentage of the most intriguing-looking young women he encountered in his travels around the city had this same sticker on their cars. So it was a pretty straightforward thing. In the lower right-hand corner of the rear window, however, was a Black Flag sticker featuring that band's well-known bars logo. This sticker, as he saw it, enhanced his goal of portraying himself as a hip, cool guy with stellar taste in underground music beyond just the newer "alternative" stuff that actually got lots of radio and MTV play. The same was true of the Dead Kennedys, Bauhaus, and Misfits stickers placed elsewhere on the rear of the vehicle. He desperately coveted Sisters of Mercy and Motorhead stickers to better complete the overall picture he was trying to convey, but had not yet been able to find any in local stores. On the rear bumper was a non-band sticker that read, *Mean People Suck*. This was another one he often saw on cars driven by cool-looking chicks and people who seemed cool in general and non-mainstream.

What he always imagined was that the stickers on his car would attract the attention of like-minded people. He pictured cool punk rocker chicks staring at the stickers while stuck behind him at a traffic light and thinking, "There's someone I might like to know. Someone not like all the lame regular dudes who only talk about football and listen to corporate rock."

Also, he spent a lot of time at Tower Records and various used music shops, and he liked to think of the people streaming in and out of the stores taking note of his stickers while his car was parked outside. He always fantasized about coming out of whichever record store he was at on any given day and being approached by some hot goth or rocker girl, one who might shyly say how much she liked his stickers before inviting him to have a drink with her.

Thus far it had not happened.

Not even once.

The hope, however, that one day it would burned eternally.

On that day in April, Cole parked his Tercel in the one available free parking space outside of Sound Stack, grabbed a cardboard box from the backseat, and went into the secondhand music shop. One of the guys behind the counter glanced at him as he came through the door, a look of slack-jawed boredom on his pale, narrow face. He had long, frizzy reddish-blond hair and a wispy goatee. His eyes had the watery, red-rimmed aspect of the perpetually stoned. The loose black Sub Pop t-shirt hanging off his gangly frame was expected. Chances were always good there was at least one of these Sub Pop t-shirt guys in any music shop. The other guy behind the counter was sitting on a stool. He was at least twice the girth of Sub Pop Guy and was wearing a Mudhoney t-shirt beneath the open front of a red flannel shirt.

Sub Pop Guy's stoned gaze didn't stay on Cole for long. At one end of the counter was a mid-sized television that appeared to be tuned to MTV during a commercial break. The guy stared at the screen and nodded his head once as if in silent affirmation of something unknown.

Cole walked up to the counter and set the box down. "Got some tapes to sell."

The guy on the stool looked at him. He had a lush mane of long brown hair and a thick beard. This combined with his size made him look sort of like a stoner lumberjack. Sighing, he rose from the stool with stultifying slowness, a deliberate and exaggerated display of how little he wanted to deal with Cole and his box of shit he no longer wanted.

After a period of what seemed like several years, he stepped up to the counter and looked down into the box. He reached inside and sorted through the tapes in a cursory way for a second or two. "This is your basic plethora of tapes. Might be maybe an hour before I have an estimate for you."

Cole tried not to groan. "An hour? Really?"

The big man shrugged. "Got a few others ahead of you."

Cole took a quick glance around. At present, there were no other customers in the store. Unless the others were all wearing cloaks of invisibility or whatever, which didn't seem likely. He made eye contact with the big man and frowned. "That's funny. I don't see anybody."

"Yeah. I know. We're kind of backed up. They're all coming back later. Unless they get sucked through a vortex into an alternate dimension, but that'll be their problem, not mine." The big man pushed a yellow notepad across the counter along with a red felt-tip pen. "Write down your name and a number where we can reach you. We'll either give you a call or you can check back in an hour. Maybe two just to be safe."

Cole scribbled down the requested info.

The estimated wait was significantly longer than he'd been hoping for, but he didn't have much choice but to accept it. He could go to one of several other secondhand music shops in the city instead, places he tended to visit multiple times a week out of lack of anything else to do, but he'd been reliably informed that Sound Stack gave a greater rate of return than those more established businesses. At least for now. They'd only been open a little over a month. Once they'd been around a little longer and came to realize how hard it'd be to move the large stock of crap they were acquiring, their rate of exchange was likely to drop. For right now, though, word was he could get forty bucks for a box of unfashionable glam metal tapes that might fetch him twenty-five elsewhere. He was jobless once again and needed to squeeze whatever extra cash he could get out of this deal.

"Guess I'll be back in an hour. Uh . . . in case I lose track of time, how late are you open?"

The big man picked up the box of tapes and set it on the floor with some others. "We close at eight on the dot. But your stuff will be safe here if you can't make it back today."

Cole glanced up at the clock mounted on the wall behind the counter, relaxing when he saw the positions of the minute and hour hands. It was still only mid-afternoon. He was at loose ends and had loads of time to kill, time he briefly considered eating up by browsing the racks of compact discs and tapes on display in the store, but the thought of loitering in this quiet place with only these guys for company was too depressing. Also depressing was the all-too-likely prospect of encountering numerous intriguing-looking CDs or tapes, none of which he could afford to purchase. Not without defeating the purpose of his trip here today.

Turning away from the counter, Cole looked out the big plate glass window at the front of the store. On the opposite side of the street, almost directly across the way from Sound Stack, was a bar called The Gold Rush. It was one of his favorite hangout places, or at least it was when he had enough spare funds to throw away on booze.

Cole frowned.

He had sixteen dollars cash in his wallet, along with a blank check. Two five-dollar bills and six wrinkly singles. The check was only for emergency purposes, in case he ran out of cash. His current checking balance was only $13.79. In a real pinch, he could pass a check for more than that, as long as he made damn sure he deposited enough to make up the difference within a day or so. He'd hit some overdraft trouble not long ago and that shit was no damn fun. Had to go begging for money from his mom and pop.

Even assuming he garnered no cash from his box of tapes—unlikely—the sixteen bucks on his person was still enough to have a beer or three at that bar and still have a little left over for gas. A more fiscally responsible person would not even entertain this notion, given his current circumstances. Spending the money on beer was also possibly a tad hypocritical in light of his reluctance to spend any portion of his paltry funds here in the music shop. At least if he bought a CD he'd have something tangible to hang on to, a real piece of property he owned. An alcoholic beverage, however, was something you possessed temporarily, often only for a few minutes, if that long. Then again, one could argue that in light of the business he was engaged in here, chances were good any purchase made at Sound Stack was also likely to be temporary.

Hmm.

Cole sighed.

The circular internal debate could go round and round forever until the end of goddamn time. Bottom line was he wanted a beer more than he wanted to heed common sense.

Before he could head across the street and have a few bottles of Rolling Rock, however, Sub Pop Guy sharply turned up the sound on the TV. An MTV news break was starting. Cole took one step away from the counter, figuring that whatever this was about was unlikely to interest him. He came to a dead stop almost as soon as Kurt Loder started talking. The music journalist sat at a small desk with a couple pieces of paper cradled in his hands like he was Walter fucking Cronkite from 1963. He spoke in a fast and matter-of-fact way that at first belied the weight of the words he was speaking. It took a few moments for the reality of it to even start to register. Cole's mouth dropped open and he had to lean against the counter to keep from falling over.

The big guy in the Mudhoney shirt said, "What did he just fucking say? Is this a joke?"

Sub Pop Guy shook his head. "I don't think it's a joke." He turned his head away from the television. He wasn't crying, but his eyes looked wetter than before in a way Cole couldn't attribute to being high. "Kurt Cobain's dead."

On the television, Kurt Loder was still yammering away. The three of them stared at the screen and only listened for the next few minutes. It was probably only because he was feeling a touch light-headed in the aftermath of the news, but for just an instant Cole was sure he felt the earth shifting beneath his feet.

The phone on the counter next to the TV started ringing.

Sub Pop Guy lifted the receiver off the cradle and put it to his ear. He listened to whoever was on the other end for a moment before he started nodding along. Then he became engaged in an animated exchange with the other person about, of course, the latest member of the dead rock star hall of fame.

The bell above the door chimed and two long-haired guys in rocker attire came into the store. One played guitar in a local band Cole had seen several times. They walked up to the counter and started babbling at the big guy in a familiar way that made it clear they were already regulars at the new shop. The subject of their discussion was the obvious thing. The same thing everybody would be talking about for days to come.

Cole walked out of the shop and into the warmth of the afternoon sun. It was the kind of day people tended to describe as "beautiful," a springtime harbinger of summer, but to Cole it didn't feel right. The world felt different than it had just a few minutes ago, and he felt a bit like a different person than the one who'd walked through that door hugging his box of tapes. He knew this was an illusion of sorts, a trick his brain was playing on him in the midst of processing unsettling news. Knowing the cold truth of a thing wasn't always what mattered most, though. He felt like he should be standing under a gloomy Seattle sky instead of basking in this heartless sunlight, but Seattle was worlds away. On the same continent, technically, but it might as well have been in another galaxy.

The black SUV with tinted windows came roaring up out of nowhere as he stepped into the street. Its tires squealed and a rear door flew open as it came to an abrupt, screeching halt.

A strong pair of hands grabbed him and hauled him into the SUV.

TWO

THE ABDUCTION HAPPENED TOO FAST and with too much ruthlessly practiced efficiency for Cole to react in any defensive way. He was shoved into the middle of the back seat and in the next instant the back door slammed shut. In another fraction of a second, the SUV was speeding away again.

The guy who'd grabbed him off the street was squeezed up against him to his left. Another guy was seated to his right, blocking any hope of escape via the opposite door. Both men were big, tall and bulky like football players whose job it was to stop pass rushers intent on decapitating their quarterback. One was white and one was a black dude who resembled Richard Roundtree in those *Shaft* movies from the 70s. Or maybe he only thought that because his real-life exposure to black people didn't amount to much, having grown up in a nearly all-white, small-town enclave. His only significant window into the lives of people of different backgrounds came via movies and music.

Tires squealed and horns honked as the big SUV blew through a crowded intersection, its backend fishtailing slightly for a moment as the vehicle narrowly avoided multiple potential collisions.

Cole craned his head around, gawking at the blur of passing traffic visible through the SUV's tinted windows. "Why are you guys going

7

so fast?"

Nobody said anything.

As several moments of ominous silence elapsed, Cole squirmed in discomfort between his two backseat captors. He felt like a small child squished in between a couple of monstrously huge and unfriendly grownups. The SUV's engine revved and roared as the silent driver took a series of sudden, sharp turns that were like getaway driver evasive maneuvers. Just like in heist movies. Only as far as Cole could tell, no one was chasing them, so it seemed a little pointless. He considered pointing this out, but decided these kidnapper guys probably didn't care about his opinion on this matter or anything else.

And then Cole thought, *Oh, shit, wait. I've been kidnapped. What the fuck?*

This made no immediate sense of any kind. He couldn't fathom any legitimate reason why anyone in the world would want to kidnap him. They couldn't ransom him for a fortune. He came from a reasonably comfortable middle-class family, but his parents were far from rich. Maybe they could come up with a few extra grand in a real pinch, but not nearly enough to make it worth anyone's while to go to this kind of trouble.

He supposed it was possible some enemy had paid these guys to snatch him as part of some elaborate revenge scheme, but he could think of no one he'd wronged severely enough to warrant anything like that. Yeah, okay, there was Davey Mullins, who'd accused him of stealing a bag of weed back in ninth grade and had stayed mad about it all through high school, despite having no proof Cole had done any such thing, but even that seemed like a stretch. Davey wasn't wrong to have suspected him, because Cole *did* steal that quarter bag, but that was going on ten damn years ago at this point.

So there was no way this was Davey's doing.

Probably.

At first Cole was too confused to feel an appropriate level of fear, but that changed as the silent minutes continued to tick by and they drove farther and farther away from the heart of the city. A host of grim possibilities began to swirl about in his head. Maybe they wanted him for reasons that had nothing to do with money or unlikely revenge scenarios. What if these guys were sickos or perverts of some kind who wanted to torture him, perhaps make him the star of an underground snuff movie? He tried telling himself this was also unlikely but derived no comfort from the thought. The truth was he didn't have the first fucking clue what was happening and even the wildest, most paranoid notions conjured by his overdriven imagination were all within the realm of possibility until he was shown otherwise.

Cole cleared his throat. "Um . . . what do you guys want with me?"

Again, his question received no response. Only stony silence.

"Because if you're planning to rob me, you should know I'm flat fucking broke, basically. I do have sixteen bucks in my wallet. It's yours if you want it, though."

Yet again, absolute silence.

No one even looked at him. They all just stared straight ahead.

There were two front seat occupants. Every now and then he caught a partial glimpse of the driver's face in the rearview mirror. He was wearing dark sunglasses and had short dark hair. The man in the passenger seat also wore dark sunglasses, as well as what looked like a black trench coat. That one sat so perfectly still it was almost like a statue was riding in the passenger seat.

Cole made a sound somewhere between a sigh and a whimper. "So, like, you guys aren't sex perverts, are you? Please tell me you're not about to rape and torture me."

This, as it turned out, was the first of his queries to elicit a response of any kind.

The black guy turned toward him and punched him in the face. Even as he recoiled from the pain, Cole immediately understood it could have been much worse. The man had pulled his punch, no doubt about it. That big ham hock of a fist looked capable of sending Superman into outer space. All he had right now was a bloody lip and what felt like the onset of a pretty serious headache. He'd be unconscious or worse if the guy had really let him have it. The punch had one clear purpose—to shut him the fuck up. The irritated look on the man's face communicated this as clearly as anything else.

Car wheels crunched over gravel.

Cole turned his head and saw they'd pulled into a construction site. In addition to a large gravel lot surrounded by a tall chain-link fence, he saw multiple trailers sitting on concrete blocks, some heavy equipment, and a row of portable toilets. Someone out there opened a gate for them, but there was no visible evidence of anyone else on the property.

That soon changed.

Directly ahead of them was an unfinished, tall building still at a relatively early stage of construction, with only a concrete foundation and a skeletal framework of girders in place. As they got closer, he saw some people standing around inside the building on what would be the bottom floor. Three more humorless-looking, thuggish men in dark clothes and sunglasses. A brown sedan—also with tinted windows—was parked outside the building.

The whole place had the look and feel of an active work site rather than a mothballed project abandoned for lack of financing, but assuming that was true, where were the workers? This time of day, with hours of sunlight left, a full crew should still be hammering away. Cole wondered if they'd been abruptly ordered off the property to give these men some privacy while they dealt with him. That would mean someone among this group of shady individuals was involved with the company charged with the construction of this building. Based on Cole's sketchy knowledge of crime stuff, derived almost entirely from movies, he could draw only one conclusion.

These guys were mafia goons.

The guess, as outrageous as it seemed on the surface, nonetheless made a degree of logical sense, fitting the limited evidence at hand. Even if this guess was on the money, however, it cleared up exactly nothing as far as Cole was concerned. What would a bunch of mob guys want with him? At no point in his thus far singularly undistinguished existence had he ever gotten himself mixed up in anything even vaguely resembling mob activity.

The SUV pulled to a stop alongside the brown sedan. Doors popped open and the goons who'd snatched him promptly exited the vehicle. The guy who'd grabbed him off the street peered inside, bending his blockish head down.

"Come on out, Tyler. Got some people who want to talk to you."

Cole gave him a blank look.

He then glanced around to see if he'd somehow overlooked another occupant of the vehicle. Someone small enough to hide away easily, even in a small, crowded space. One of Santa's elves, perhaps. Or a toddler. One named Tyler. His search, unsurprisingly, turned up nothing of the sort.

The goon snapped his fingers. "Hey, I'm talking to you. Do I have to drag you out of there?"

Cole frowned. "I think you guys have mistaken me for someone else. My name isn't Tyler. It's Cole. Cole Watson."

The man sighed. "Let me give you a piece of advice. Lay off the bullshit when you speak to the man in charge here. You're not getting out of this and you'll only make things worse for yourself by spewing a bunch of lies."

Cole made a sound of deep exasperation. "But I'm *not* lying. I don't know who this Tyler motherfucker is, I swear. You've got the wrong guy."

Of course.

There it was. The real explanation for all of this. Your basic, classic case of mistaken identity. It was so obvious now, but so far these scary assholes remained oblivious to the truth. Somehow he had to make them understand before it was too late, because he was getting the sense this mysterious Tyler dude had done something profoundly stupid.

A colossal mistake of some kind.

One Cole was maybe about to pay for with his life.

The big goon scowled. "Fuck it. Dragging it is."

Seconds later, Cole was out of the vehicle and flying through the air. He hit the ground hard and coughed, gagging on gravel dust.

THREE

A PAIR OF STRONG HANDS grabbed hold of Cole and hauled him off the ground. He gasped in pain as the same goon twisted an arm behind his back, steered him toward the unfinished building and pushed him forward. Stumbling along and still somewhat stunned from his rough impact with the ground, only the strength of the man pinning his arm back kept him upright. The other goons from the SUV walked with them and soon they were all standing beneath the metal framework of the building-in-progress.

Of the three men who'd arrived ahead of them, one was clearly the leader. This was a fortyish dude. He had perfectly-styled hair with a lot of gel in it and wore a suit tailored for his trim body. It looked expensive. So did the large gold ring adorning his left ring finger. The guy reminded him of someone. At first he had trouble identifying who he was thinking of, but then it came to him.

"Pat Riley."

The stylish man frowned. "What?"

"The coach of the L.A. Lakers. You could be his twin."

The man's frown turned into a sneer. "A joker. I don't have time for jokes and neither do you. Smart remarks are not good for your health. Okay? You got that?"

Cole nodded. "I'm sorry. There's been some kind of misunderstanding here. I'm not—"

The Pat Riley doppelganger cut him off with an abrupt hand gesture. "Hurt him."

His arm was released and an instant later a hard punch drilled into his lower back, blasting the air from his lungs and driving him to his knees. He was still wheezing and gasping for breath when he was jerked back to his feet and shaken a time or two like a ragdoll. He felt like he'd been hit in the back with the business end of a sledgehammer. This was pain he'd still be feeling vestiges of days from now, if he lived that long, which didn't feel like a safe assumption at this point.

The rest of them listened in silence for several seconds while Cole whimpered and tried his best to think of the right combination of words that would finally convince these people they'd made a terrible mistake.

Then the black dude who'd punched him in the SUV glanced over at him and said, "Riley coaches the Knicks now."

The stylish man scowled. "Did I ask for a sporting news update, Mr. ESPN? No, I did not."

The black dude grimaced. "Sorry, Mr. Russell."

The heels of Russell's polished businessman shoes clicked on the cement floor as he stepped closer. He didn't stop until Cole could feel the man's minty breath on his face. "Let's cut the crap, Tyler. You took something that doesn't belong to you. Something important from the files of Arthur Jamison. That was a stupid thing to do, but you have a chance to make things right. Your *last* chance. So where is it, Tyler? Where is the microfiche?"

Cole ceased blubbering long enough to say, "The what?"

Russell slapped him hard enough to leave a scarlet imprint of fingers on one side of his face. "The microfiche, you obfuscating piece of shit! Where is it?"

Russell's underlings all exchanged grim-faced glances, which was not exactly reassuring.

Cole cleared phlegm from his throat a couple times before attempting speech again. "I'm sorry, and let me just say in advance I know this won't be what you want to hear, but I swear to God it's the absolute truth. I have no goddamn idea what the hell you're talking about." He enunciated each word of that last sentence in an exaggeratedly deliberate way, hoping it would make obvious the true scope of his ignorance. "So please help me understand. What's so important about a miniature fishie?"

Stunned silence for a moment.

Then an abrupt and short-lived snort of laughter from one of the goons.

Russell's eyes narrowed to slits and his bottom lip began to quiver, slowly at first, almost imperceptibly, but then in a steadily more noticeable way as his rage continued to build. The line of his jaw looked razor-sharp beneath his skin as he clenched his teeth and made some deeply scary noises. He sounded like some wild beast on the verge of devouring cornered prey.

Cole felt close to pissing his pants.

Russell turned away from him and took several rapid strides in the opposite direction, roughly shouldering his way between two of the goons. Aggression building toward an explosion of violence was evident in his every step. He stopped and turned his head skyward, unleashing a scream of fury.

After the sound trailed off, he spent several additional moments facing away from Cole until he collected himself. He looked almost calm again when he finally turned back around. There was even a faint hint of a smile at the edges of his mouth as he came closer. Unlike the last time, he stopped well short of getting right up in Cole's face, for which his captive was briefly grateful, until he began to wonder whether it portended some other form of impending violence.

Cole sniffled.

Oh, fuck, am I about to be shot?

He hadn't seen any guns yet, but he assumed several were present, hidden away beneath trench coats and jackets.

Cole began to openly weep.

Russell eyed each member of the kidnapping team in turn, the ghost of a smile remaining in place while his dark eyes conveyed only a ruthless coldness. "Am I correct in assuming one of you searched the young idiot before bringing him here? There's no chance he has the item on his person?"

Nobody said anything. Words weren't necessary. The looks on the faces of the kidnappers said it all.

Russell sighed. "Jesus suffering Christ. Do it now, please."

The goon Cole thought of as Street Snatcher let go of his arm and commenced an embarrassingly invasive full body search. His crotch hadn't gotten this much attention since the last time he'd gotten a lap dance at a strip club. It was embarrassing, but he had no choice but to endure the violation. He felt his wallet leave the back pocket of his jeans and figured he'd never see those sixteen bucks in wrinkly bills again.

Done groping him at last, Street Snatcher said, "Don't think he has it on him. Well . . . unless it's shoved up his ass."

Some of the other goons snickered.

Russell smirked. "Drop your pants, kid. You're about to get the full prison bitch treatment." He chuckled. "Unless you're finally ready to cut the shit and give up the microfiche."

Ominous words, but hearing the man say "micro feesh" again temporarily overrode any increase in fear he might otherwise have experienced. He couldn't figure out why the stylish psychopath kept pronouncing fish in such a bizarre way. The way a toddler might say it. It'd be cute spilling out of the mouth of a mini-human waddling around in a fucking onesie, but not so much in this case. He was about to say as much when a foggy memory from his high school days floated into his head, one that might've made him laugh under other circumstances. Instead it just made him want to cry.

Microfiche, not "micro feesh."

Aka microfilm.

For fuck's sake.

Not that this belated moment of recognition really changed anything.

He didn't have the thing the dude was looking for.

"Hold on a minute." That was Street Snatcher speaking again. "Uh, I don't think this is the guy we were supposed to grab."

Cole turned and looked at him.

Street Snatcher had his pilfered wallet open and was looking at his driver's license. "ID says this guy's name is Cole Watson. Not Tyler Barnes."

Scowling, the black dude snatched the wallet away from his partner and removed the ID from its plastic sleeve. The wallet slipped from his fingers and hit cement. His scowl deepened as he examined the license before softening into a look of a more sheepish nature. It was the look of a man who knows he has fucked up on an almost irredeemable level. "Aw, shit. This ain't the guy. We got the wrong mother trucker."

He took a Polaroid photograph from an inner pocket of his jacket and held it up next to the license, squinting as he spent several exasperated moments examining both.

Russell brushed past Cole and took the photo and license away from his henchman. After several seconds of intensely scrutinizing both items, his face began to twist with rage. "There is a superficial resemblance, but what I'm seeing is two distinctly different white boys with long hair." He laughed, but the sound had a harsh edge to it. "What a colossal goddamn fuckup. What an absolute disaster. How could this possibly have happened?"

All four members of the kidnapping team started fidgeting in noticeable ways, shifting their weight around and grimacing. Their faces glistened with sweat. The guy who'd been the front seat passenger, the one in the black trench coat, was the first to buckle in the face of the boss man's fury. He reached inside the trench coat and whipped out a semi-auto pistol.

Cole yelped in fright as a shot rang out.

FOUR

BLOOD FLEW FROM THE BACK of Trench Coat Guy's head as a dime-sized hole appeared in the center of his forehead. A second later, his body was on the cement floor, more blood spreading out in a steadily widening pool around his head. His kidnapping team co-horts stood as still as statues, their eyes wide with terror and shock. These other men almost certainly had weapons of their own hidden inside their own jackets, but they were not quite stupid enough to reach for them. It'd be an instant death sentence. Russell's other men—the ones who'd been waiting here with him—already had their guns out and pointed. One wrong move, even a questionable twitch, would be ill-advised.

Cole felt his bowels twist as he stared at the dead man. The de-structive power of that single bullet was a sickening thing. He'd seen a million Hollywood movies filled with bad guys and good guys shooting each other and throwing around an exorbitant amount of lead, but nothing captured on celluloid had adequately prepared him for the ugly reality of a man being shot to death right in front of him. Seeing it happen had a devastating impact on his already fragile psy-che. More than pretty much anything else in the world, he didn't want to wind up like the man on the floor, with his blood and brains leaking out of a hole, robbed of everything that made him uniquely human in the time it took to squeeze a trigger And yet he couldn't help feeling like he was already doomed, even now that these criminal bastards had realized their mistake.

Cole started talking, driven by desperation and terror, blubbering and rambling on about his desperate desire to go on living. He swore he'd forget all about this incident and never breathe a word of it to anyone. They had nothing to fear from him. He was a useless piece of shit no one anywhere took seriously anyway. And after all, he still didn't truly know what any of this was about. So, okay, they were after a piece of microfilm. Big deal. He wasn't a fucking psychic. He didn't know what was on the goddamn thing, and he was no threat to whatever secret they were trying to protect

Russell backhanded him. "Not another word from you, punk. I mean it. I don't ever want to hear your pathetic whining voice again."

The man's attention returned to the now reduced squad of bumbling kidnappers. "As for you fucking imbeciles, you have one chance to make things right and one chance only."

Street Snatcher replied in a tone so obsequious and desperate it was pathetic. "You can count on us, Mr. Russell. We won't let you down again." He raised a hand like a man being sworn in as a court witness. "I swear it on my mother's grave. We'll get the right guy this time."

Russell snorted derisive laughter. "No, you won't. If you think I'd entrust you clowns with that job again, you're even stupider than you look. This time I'm sending only the best, my top guys, which is what I should've done in the first fucking place. No, what you need to do is clean up this mess. Make that sack of meat with the hole where his brains used to be disappear without a fucking trace." He hooked a thumb in Cole's direction. "And while you're at it, get rid of this mental midget, too. Do all that without fucking it up and maybe you'll live to see another day. Maybe."

He smirked as he and his bodyguards started walking away.

~

Everyone kept their mouths shut as Russell departed with his goons.

Everyone except Russell himself, who snorted and muttered something that sounded like, "Miniature fishies. Jesus Christ."

Russell and his men all piled into the brown sedan and drove away.

A silent beat elapsed during which everyone who remained stood stock-still. The eyes of the kidnappers were all directed at their dead partner. The tension gripping them was like a living thing, a poison-ous snake coiling in their guts. It didn't break until the bearded man who'd driven the SUV let out a loud moan and staggered away from the rest of them. He bent over at the waist and braced his hands on his knees as he vomited onto the dusty cement floor.

Street Snatcher and the black dude visibly relaxed and let out loud exhalations of relief. These were followed by numerous agitated dec-larations of disbelief and anger. The disbelief was largely centered around the genuine grief they were feeling at the loss of their cohort. At that point Cole realized these men weren't just paid thugs who worked together. There were real friendships involved here. Perhaps that could work to his advantage. If these men were capable of expe-riencing real empathy, maybe he had a chance.

The black dude reached inside his jacket and came out with a pis-tol he immediately aimed at Cole's head.

"No, wait!" Cole dropped to his knees and held his hands clasped in front of him, lifted high like an inveterate sinner begging God for forgiveness at the last possible moment. "You don't have to kill me. I'll never tell a soul about any of this."

A pained look crossed the man's face. "Sorry. I don't want to do this, but I got no choice. You heard what the man said."

Tears streamed down Cole's face as he clasped his hands tighter together. "But that's just it. I did hear what your boss said and he didn't say a word about murdering me. Think back. All he said was to get rid of me."

Street Snatcher grunted. "Huh. I mean, he ain't wrong. Not tech-nically. Boss man didn't actually say to kill him. Maybe we should just remove the kid from the premises and drop him off somewhere."

The black dude gave him a dubious look. "Come on, man. Mr. Russell might not have explicitly said to put a bullet in this dumb mother trucker's head, but we all know what he meant when he said get rid of him."

The bearded driver was done heaving now. He stood up straight and turned to address the rest of them. "George is right. Boss man didn't say it, but it was implied. We already fucked up big-time once today. Do we really want to risk making Mr. Russell even angrier by deciding to creatively misinterpret his words? Because I think we all know what would happen if he found out."

Cole began to openly sob, knowing for sure he was doomed now. There would be no talking his way out of this, nor would there be some miraculous last-minute rescue. No one who cared about him was even aware of his dire predicament. Having resigned himself to the absolute futile hopelessness of his situation, Cole toppled over onto his side with his hands still clasped together. He curled up in a fetal ball and commenced to wailing like a baby. Screwing his eyes shut as tight as they'd go, he tried hard to make his mind go blank, to blot out all awareness of the impending doom about to descend on him.

Several moments passed.

Someone said, "Damned if this ain't the most pitiful thing I've ever seen." The deep voice was immediately identifiable as belonging to the man he now knew was named George. Such an ordinary-sounding moniker for a big, scary dude who vaguely resembled a 70s blaxploitation star. It was the name of a regular guy. A blue-collar working stiff, not some killer. "I'm embarrassed on your behalf, kid."

Cole unleashed another loud wail of abject misery.

"I don't know if I can be a part of this," Street Snatcher interjected. "It'd be like killing a puppy. I don't know about the rest of you, but that's not me. I'm no saint, mind you, but I'm no heartless scumbag either."

George grimaced. "Goddammit."

He stomped away from the rest of them and spent some time venting a mounting frustration over the situation. Building materials and various pieces of construction equipment went flying about, clanging off girders and skidding across the cement floor. He kicked a steel barrel full of debris so hard it toppled over and rolled until it hit a stack of bricks. In his frenzy, he got a foot caught in a loosely coiled power cable and took a tumble. His friends raced over to check on him as he cursed in voluminous and colorful fashion and tried kicking free of the cable.

By then, Cole's eyes were open again and he wondered if he should make a run for it. He sat up and craned his head around, looking for his wallet. Money for a cab would be a good thing to have in the wildly unlikely event he did get away from these guys. At first he thought it was probably still in Street Snatcher's possession, but then he spied it on the floor several feet away, right at the edge of the pool of blood surrounding the dead man's head. His discarded driver's license was a few feet further away.

Glancing at the kidnappers and seeing that they were still distracted, he scurried over on his hands and knees to retrieve his property. The wallet dripped blood from a corner as he picked it up. Feeling queasy, he grabbed his license and quickly shoved both items into his back pocket. On impulse, without having a clue why he should want it, he hurriedly scooped up the Polaroid of Tyler Barnes and shoved it into the same pocket.

The bearded driver glanced over at him and frowned. "The fuck are you doing?"

Cole made his eyes go round as he tried his best to look innocent. "Um . . . nothing."

The driver's frown deepened. "Uh-huh. Well, stop moving around. We haven't settled anything with you yet."

Cole nodded. "Okay."

By the time George was finally back on his feet and free of the cable, he looked ready to blow a gasket. Cole trembled as the man's furious gaze settled on him again. He spent several seconds convinced the man's apparent crisis of conscience was over and that he would soon put a bullet in his skull after all.

Then the big man's expression softened again. "Look, son, I know you wound up in this shitty predicament through no fault of your own. It's *our* fault, but we can't take back our mistake. Which isn't fair. Not one goddamn bit. But you know what? Life's just that way sometimes." He glanced at Street Snatcher. "What about you, Hollis? Has life been fair to you? Do you get up in the morning and say to yourself, 'Damn, things have worked out really well for me, and I am just as happy as a pig in shit?'"

Hollis—aka Street Snatcher—shook his head. "I do not."

The driver chuckled. "Me either."

George pointed the gun directly at Cole's head again. "That's right. Things don't always work out and life is one cruel bitch. So, kid, unless you can think of a solid gold fantastic fucking reason why I should let you live, one that gets us all off the hook with the boss man, I'm afraid this is the end of the road for you."

Cole's heart started pounding again, but to his surprise the tears did not resume flowing. "I . . . I . . . fuck, I can't think of anything."

George nodded. "That's because the magic words you're looking for do not exist. I'm sorry. I hate this, brother. I really do."

Once again, Cole shut his eyes tight and awaited the end.

FIVE

THE NEXT THING COLE EXPECTED to hear was the roar of a gunshot, but that did not immediately happen. He figured the man who intended to act as his executioner was still working up the nerve to commit murder. Enough time passed for him to realize he'd probably never hear the gunshot anyway. He didn't know the actual mathematics or science of it, but he knew bullets traveled at immense speed. The projectile would pass through his head before his ears even had a chance to process the sound.

He opened his eyes when he heard a metallic click. What he saw then surprised the hell out of him. Hollis had his own gun out now and was pointing it at the side of his friend's head.

"Drop the gun, George."

George stared straight ahead, keeping his gun raised and pointed, still poised to deliver a point-blank shot to the center of Cole's face. "What do you think you're doing, man? Have you lost your mind?"

Hollis sighed. "I said it once already. I can't be a part of anything like this. Intimidation I can do. Threats I can do. Go rough up somebody who owes the boss money? Yeah, I can do that, too. But I didn't sign up for murdering innocent people. We ain't the mob. Not like for real, anyway."

The driver eyed Hollis in what struck Cole as a coldly calculating way. As he watched the man's right hand creep slowly toward the inside of his open jacket, Cole realized his survival beyond the next few seconds would require him to stop acting like a spectator in a movie theater and actually do something. For someone whose default setting in life was bored passivity, this did not come easily. By the time he was finally able to overcome this mental hurdle, the driver's hand was fully inside his jacket.

"Hey, Hollis."

The man's gaze remained riveted to the side of George's head. "Yeah, kid?"

"That other dude's reaching for his gun."

Hollis looked at the driver. His gun swung in that direction an instant later. "That hand better be empty when it comes out of your jacket, Frank. And don't even think about doing anything dumb while I'm dealing with this shit, George. I've still got the drop on you."

George chuckled. "I'm not the one doing dumb shit, brother. How many years do we go back? Eight or nine? Almost a damn decade. You expect me to believe you'd choose to kill your friends just to save some punk you never met before today?"

The look on Hollis's face was regret tinged with determination. "Goddammit, George, have I not made myself clear? I'd rather not shoot anybody. But right is right and wrong is wrong. And you know what? This shit has been coming to a head for a long time. I'm done doing dirty work for that fancy scumbag. This is it. My line in the sand."

George turned around and pointed his gun at Hollis.

Cole almost fainted.

Hollis didn't even flinch.

George said, "So what's your plan? Get a regular job and punch a time clock instead of deadbeats?"

Hollis shrugged. "Something like that, yeah."

Frank smirked as his empty hand slowly came out of his jacket. "Sounds boring. I'd rather be a crook than a slave to the system."

Hollis nodded. "No judgment on you guys. Look, put all this on me. Tell Russell I ambushed you guys. You never saw it coming. I drove off with the kid and you have no idea where I went. You said it yourself, man. This isn't what you want. Killing this fucking kid. Well, this is how you get out of doing it and still get to stay on Russell's payroll. So . . . what do you think?"

George grunted. "I can see you've given this a lot of thought. There's some things that have been weighing on you for a long time. And I appreciate that. I truly do. But the answer is no."

His gun boomed and a bullet punched a hole through the bridge of Hollis's nose.

SIX

THE DRIVER, FRANK, GASPED IN shock as the big man dropped like a sack of rocks. He put a hand to his chest and immediately made another sound evoking an intense level of disbelief.

Cole empathized.

Contrary to anything he would have guessed possible, one of the bad guys had emerged as a potential savior. The very one who'd grabbed him off the street, in fact. A guy who maybe wasn't such a bad guy after all. At least not entirely. But now, after a heartfelt speech expressing a sentiment Cole stupidly began to believe would carry the day, he was dead at the hand of his so-called friend, taking all hope of salvation with him.

Frank's eyes brimmed with tears. "Jesus, George. You blew Hollis's fucking brains out! What the hell?"

George glanced at him. "Get a grip, man. You think I wanted to do that? I fucking did not. But his mind was set. I saw it in the mother trucker's eyes. There wasn't gonna be any talking him out of that moronic scheme. Think about what that would've meant for you and me. How weak we would've looked in Mr. Russell's eyes for letting something like that happen. We're already on his shit list for grabbing the wrong dude. That shit would've been a death sentence for both of us.

You know I'm right."

His tone was aggressive and emphatic, as if were trying to convince himself as much as his one remaining friend. Despite the dire implications it held for him, Cole found it difficult to disagree with the basic truth of what the man was saying.

Frank was still distraught, still gasping and wheezing with his hand to his chest.

George huffed in frustration. "Come on, man! Get it together. Let's finish this nasty business and get on with our goddamn lives." His attention shifted back to Cole, aiming the gun at his head again. "This shit's on me for hesitating, for ever letting you get under our skin. You're bad luck, kid."

A higher-pitched whine issued from Frank as he dropped to one knee.

Cole frowned. "Something's wrong with your friend."

George sneered. "Nuh-uh. I'm done letting you mess with my head."

Frank wheezed one last time and fell over, landing on his side before rolling onto his back.

"Shit!"

George hurried over to his friend, dropping to a knee at his side. He started yelling at him and slapping his face, urging him to wake up. What good that was supposed to do, Cole did not know. An attempt at CPR was probably called for here. At the very least. What the man really needed was an ambulance and a trip to the hospital, but that obviously wasn't in the cards. At last, George surrendered to reality, set his gun down, and started pounding on Frank's chest. Cole was no expert by any means, but even he could see this was far removed from any standard, medically approved method of resuscitation.

He realized the man's moment of distraction wouldn't last much longer. This was a guy who'd already shot one of his best pals point blank in the fucking face, after all. Cole scanned the immediate vicinity in desperate search of some means of deliverance from his dilemma.

His breath caught in his throat when he saw the thing he hoped would save him.

Trying hard to make as little noise as possible, he picked up the cinder block, moved up behind George, and slammed it down on his head.

SEVEN

A SICK FEELING ASSAILED COLE as he felt the crunch of impact and heard the sharp splintering of bone. The sick feeling redoubled as he lifted the cinder block again and saw the pulped mess created by the single, heavy blow. George's head was partly caved in at the crown of his skull. Blood welled out of the newly created cranial opening, which also allowed a glimpse of what Cole assumed was the man's brain.

As devastating as the blow was, it didn't quite finish the job. George's body shook as he made a horrible series of indecipherable sputtering sounds. He tried turning his head toward Cole, but this only intensified the tremors gripping his body. His hand spasmed like a live electrical wire knocked down by a storm as he tried reaching for his gun.

Cole couldn't believe it.

The guy had a big-ass hole in his head and his will to fight and survive was refusing to give in to the obvious. His hand dropped closer to the floor, hovering an inch above the gun. In his current state, it was impossible to imagine him managing to grip and effectively wield the weapon.

But why take the chance?

Cole raised the cinder block and brought it down again. The damage inflicted by the second blow was even more catastrophic than the first, flattening the top of the kidnapper's head.

George fell over and ceased shaking.

Still gripping his chosen tool of destruction, Cole stared at the man's ruined head in a state of numb disbelief for several moments. That was a real thing he'd done. He understood this as objective fact, but a protective part of his psyche went into denial overdrive. During those moments, the grisly visual evidence of what had transpired didn't *feel* real. It was like something out of a splatter movie, special makeup effects by Tom Savini. Because how did it make sense that it was anything other than an illusion? He wasn't a violent person, aside from being involved in a few half-hearted bar scuffles. His opponents in those altercations were all similarly unskilled in the art of kicking ass and no lasting damage was ever done. In most such cases, everyone was laughing about it the next day. Or, sometimes, even just a few minutes later.

This was different.

There'd be no laughing off any of it later. These men were *dead*.

Cole felt his gorge rising as he began to come out of that initial numb state. After dropping the cinder block, he turned away from the sight of George's pancaked skull and staggered over to a stack of bricks. He braced a hand against it and vomited as he bent over at the waist. His guts continuously clenched and twisted for several moments. It was the most severe episode of gastrointestinal distress he'd experienced since that time he got high and consumed an entire jar of jalapeno slices while watching an episode of *Beavis and Butthead*. Early the next morning he dug the jar out of the trash and examined it until he discovered a stamped expiration date of nearly a year in the past.

In truth, what he was experiencing now, while bad, wasn't quite *that* bad. He wasn't sure a non-fatal level of sickness beyond what he'd gone through that time was even possible.

At last the heaving subsided and he stood up straight again.

After taking a few extra moments to mentally steel himself, he moved away from the stack of bricks and spent some time surveying the tableau of death the building's unfinished floor had become. This time he was able to accept the gruesome reality of it all, though that made it no less surreal. Only a few minutes ago these men were alive and seemingly in firm control of his fate. Now, on the other side of a bizarre and unlikely string of events, they were all dead.

And Cole was not.

He didn't know whether to laugh or cry. Depending on how you looked at it, in this moment right here and now, he was either the luckiest or unluckiest son of a bitch on the entire goddamn planet. Perhaps in all of existence, throughout all the known and unknown parts of the universe.

Lucky or not, it wouldn't be wise to linger here much longer.

The SUV that had conveyed him to this place was still parked outside the skeletal building. His next move was obvious. Take the keys off Frank and get the hell gone. He didn't know exactly where he was, but it didn't matter. Only escape mattered.

Cole moved to the opposite side of the supine driver—the side without the corpse of a man with a bashed-in head lying next to it—and squatted, leaning over him to dig into his hip pocket. The lump he saw in the fabric made it obvious the keys were there. His hand was just closing around several little slivers of metal when Frank let out a gasp and tried to sit up.

Cole felt like quite possibly the dumbest person who'd ever lived. *Of course* he should've checked Frank for a pulse instead of simply assuming the man had expired from the apparent cardiac event. Sure, he could blame the oversight on an overload of intense psychological trauma, but that didn't make it any less dumb or careless.

His hand came out of Frank's pocket with the keys gripped tight in his fingers.

"What's . . . going . . . on?" Frank struggled to speak between wheezing gasps, his eyes wide with fear and bleary with confusion. He cried out in distress when he saw what had happened to George's head. "Oh, Jesus! Georgie! What did you do?"

Cole's mouth moved, but no words emerged.

What could he say that wouldn't upset this man?

Not a damn thing.

On impulse, he snatched George's gun off the floor and pointed the barrel at Frank's gaping mouth. A low whine, nearly inaudible at first, began issuing from the open cavity. It grew louder, becoming more like the whistling of a tea kettle. Then the sound abruptly ceased and the man clutched at his chest with both hands before flopping backward again.

Cole gaped at him a moment before saying, "Um . . . dude? Are you okay?"

No response.

Frank's eyes were open and unmoving. He didn't blink.

This time Cole did check for a pulse. There wasn't one.

Well, shit.

It seemed he'd scared the guy to death.

He felt bad about it. It wasn't a thing he'd done with deliberate deadly intent, unlike, obviously, what he'd done to George. He'd only wanted to intimidate the man into not making any sudden moves against him. As a consequence of frightening him into the great beyond, that goal had been achieved.

Cole got shakily to his feet and began staggering away from the scene of carnage. He stopped in his tracks before reaching the SUV, however, and turned back, gripped by another wild impulse. Delaying his exit any longer probably wasn't smart, but the impulse overwhelmed his self-preserving instincts. This was something his gut told him he needed to do, even if the extra time it took elevated his level of risk.

He checked the wallets of the dead men and extracted a significant wad of cash. Hundreds of dollars. A lot of the bills were hardly wrinkled at all. It was the most money he'd seen all at once in a long, long time. He shoved it all into his pockets, retrieved George's gun, and finally drove away from what he'd decided to think of as *The Construction Site of the Damned.*

EIGHT

GETTING BACK TO MORE FAMILIAR territory proved considerably less difficult than he'd feared. A stop at a gas station to ask for directions was all it took. A scant ten minutes later, he began to see buildings he recognized.

The music shop was in a small entertainment district not far from the big local university for rich kids. Elliston Place was home to a diverse collection of shops, bars, and music venues. Students and other dedicated drinkers packed the area on weekend nights, transforming the ordinarily quiet street into a wild and vibrant nightlife scene. It was late afternoon on a Friday, which meant things would start getting hectic before much longer, so the sooner he could make it back over there to retrieve his car, the better he'd feel about things.

After ditching the SUV a couple streets over, Cole began making his way back to the scene of his abduction, proceeding at a rapid clip while trying not to appear overly agitated. This was not an easy proposition. He wasn't a carefree ordinary citizen out for a lazy, late afternoon stroll. Outwardly he looked the same as ever, like a harmless suburban stoner dude, but inside he was a man transformed. A killer. Didn't matter how crazy it was to think of himself that way. It was the plain fucking truth. He was a head-basher and a skull-cracker. A terror-inducer. A heart-stopper and a robber of corpses. There was a semi-automatic pistol shoved into the waistband of his jeans and he felt like he was walking in a noticeably funny way because of it. At least the untucked hem of his tie-dyed shirt effectively hid the protruding pistol butt. Or so he hoped. But what if the outline of it was visible to anyone walking behind him?

Fuck!

That was a possibility he hadn't considered.

Taking the gun with him as he fled the construction site had seemed a prudent thing to do at the time, but now having it on his person was causing him serious anxiety. He still thought having some means of defending himself should he encounter more of Russell's hired goons was a solid idea, despite harboring some doubt regarding his ability to effectively wield the thing. Guns seemed easy in theory. Point and shoot. But he'd never actually fired one and suspected that in actual practice it might not be so simple. At least he'd worked out how to engage the safety and didn't have to worry about the fucking thing going off in his pants. Shooting yourself in the ass was the kind of thing where, even if you survived it, you'd never hear the end of it, and he got enough grief from his asshole friends as it was.

His anxiety level started going up again as he neared Church Street. The street corner was another twenty feet straight ahead. A left turn there and The Gold Rush bar would be only two blocks away, and at that point he'd be directly across the street from the spot where he'd been snatched.

He stopped in his tracks and frowned.

There must have been some reason the kidnapping occurred at that particular spot. The way it turned out, they'd grabbed the wrong guy, but no way had it happened where it did by random chance. They must have had good cause to think they'd run into Tyler Barnes at that specific time and location. Would Russell's second kidnapping team—his so-called "top" guys—return to the same spot to try again? Might they be in the vicinity even now, waiting for Barnes to materialize?

Shit.

The possibility was one he desperately wished he could dismiss, but logic suggested that would be a mistake. Barnes probably worked in the area, perhaps in one of the several other shops in the same two-story building that was home to Sound Stack. Or in one of the bars or music venues. He hadn't recognized the guy in the Polaroid, but that didn't mean anything. He came out to Elliston Place maybe a couple times a month, not nearly often enough to know everyone who worked up and down the street by sight. The second kidnapping team *probably* wouldn't make the same mistake as the first, but Cole wasn't willing to bet his life on it.

Getting back to his car was the central issue here in more ways than one. It didn't merely represent his easiest means of getting back home. He didn't want to leave it in that same spot overnight and risk returning sometime tomorrow to find it'd been towed.

After fretting about it a bit longer, an idea came to him.

A few blocks up Church Street, in the opposite direction of Sound Stack, was a big Exxon gas station and convenience store. He'd stopped in there for last-minute beer a few times after last call at The Gold Rush. There were some things there that might be of use in getting him out of this dilemma.

He hurried to the corner, turned up Church Street, and started walking that way.

NINE

TAKING CARE OF BUSINESS AT the gas station was weird but
not overly complicated. Cole spent some time browsing merchandise
in the store, mostly looking at items meant to tempt drunken tourists.
After making his selections and paying at the counter, he went to the
bathroom and locked himself in a stall for a few minutes.

The clerks on duty did a double-take the next time they saw him,
then glanced at each other with raised eyebrows. He was no longer
wearing the tie-dyed shirt. It was stuffed deep inside a waste bin in
the bathroom. In its place was a black Johnny Cash shirt. His long
hair was now pulled back in a ponytail and secured with a purple hair
tie. Cheap mirrored sunglasses hid his eyes and atop his head was an
orange UT baseball hat.

He gave the guys at the counter a nod and walked on out of the
store. The looks on their faces said they knew something was a little
off about him, but he'd paid for his wardrobe transformation instead
of shoplifting, so who were they to say anything?

The cobbled together disguise was the best he could do with the
limited resources available at the gas station. He'd given some
thought to getting a Magic Marker to draw a fake mustache above his
upper lip, but in the end he decided it'd be best to keep things as

simple as possible. He also suspected a ridiculous drawn-on mustache would only succeed at drawing more attention his way.

After coming out of the gas station, he again walked up the sidewalk until he arrived at the corner of Church and 16th. The area was getting busier now, with more cars flowing through the intersection and an increase in foot traffic. Things would really start hopping in about another hour, when it started getting dark. He hoped to be long gone before then.

A gap in traffic opened and he hurried across to the opposite corner. A handful of other fast-moving pedestrians accompanied him. A youngish mixed group of men and women he at first figured were older than him by at least a few years. A moment's closer scrutiny, however, made him realize he was their age or pretty close. They just *looked* older because they dressed in a more upwardly mobile fashion. Recognizing this made him a little uncomfortably self-conscious.

He was constantly being told he needed to grow up and start acting his age. Maybe there was something to that. He was in his midtwenties and not getting any younger. Hell, at a month away from turning twenty-seven, even self-identifying as being in his *mid*-twenties wouldn't be accurate for much longer. What if he continued living the way he did for a few more years, until he was in his fucking thirties? It seemed to him there was a thin line between being a young slacker taking his sweet time figuring out his place in the world and just becoming an actual bum. What if it was already too late for him to change?

This was some heavy shit to ponder under any circumstances, but it could prove fatally distracting for someone in his situation. He put it out of his head and continued scanning both sides of the street as he slowly moved up the sidewalk, but so far he wasn't seeing anything that set off any alarms. The increase in foot traffic also helped ease his anxiety. This wasn't like earlier in the afternoon, when the street had been virtually empty. He had a hard time imagining anyone being brazen enough to try something like that again with so many witnesses around. While this was somewhat reassuring, he wasn't ready to let his guard down quite yet.

The Gold Rush was still a block away when he glanced to the other side of the street again and got his first unobstructed look at his car. A wave of relief swept over him. He hadn't been gone long enough to warrant anyone putting in a call to a tow company. This was something he'd known on a rational level anyway, but that didn't matter with paranoia coloring his every thought. Until just now, a big part of him was convinced the car would be gone, and seeing it still there waiting for him right where he'd left it had him on the verge of tears.

Even better, there was no sign whatsoever of anyone shady-looking lingering near the Tercel.

Rather than continuing up the street, he stepped between two cars parked at the curb and waited for another gap in traffic to open. He would have to move fast because gaps he could slip through without getting squashed by an oncoming vehicle were occurring less frequently.

He waited, growing impatient.

A small gap opened and he ran.

A horn blared and someone yelled at him through an open window, but he nonetheless managed to arrive safely at the other side of the street. His heart was racing as he stepped up to the sidewalk and continued walking in the direction of Sound Stack. He gave the vicinity another careful scan as he arrived in the parking lot outside the little shopping center, turning in a full circle to take in the other side of the street as well.

Still no sign of lurking evildoers or anything else obviously amiss.

He dug out his keys as he approached his car. His box of tapes was still in the music shop, but he decided he'd either return for them another time or simply abandon them. Lingering even one second longer than absolutely necessary didn't seem like a good idea. He felt relatively safe at the moment, but he couldn't count on that remaining the case.

His hand was trembling as his keys came clear of his hip pocket, and as a result his first few attempts at jabbing the Tercel's key into the door lock were unsuccessful. He muttered a variety of curses as the key scraped the burgundy paint multiple times. In his peripheral vision, he glimpsed someone approaching from the direction of the music shop.

His breath caught in his throat as he turned his head and glanced that way.

"Holy shit."

It was him.

Motherfucking Tyler Barnes.

TEN

THE GUY GAVE HIM A funny look and stopped short of moving past him.

"Something wrong, man?"

Cole blinked rapidly behind the mirrored shades. "Um . . . no?"

Barnes smirked. "You don't sound too sure about that. Why did you say 'holy shit' when you saw me?"

Cole shrugged. "Thought of something random. Nothing to do with you."

"Whatever, man. Could you step out of the fucking way, please?"

"Sure. Sorry."

Cole put his back against the Tercel as Barnes moved on by him in the narrow space between cars. He turned and watched the guy go as he continued on across the street, racing through another of those small gaps in traffic. It was crazy how he was out walking around in public like someone without a worry in the world instead of hiding out somewhere. Once Barnes was on the other side, he headed straight for The Gold Rush. He disappeared through the entrance a moment later.

This complicated things on multiple annoying levels. He cursed the rotten luck of his timing. If he'd spent even one less minute dithering about in the gas station, he'd likely be in his car and on his way home now, blissfully unaware of a narrowly avoided encounter with Barnes. Instead he'd arrived right on time to directly cross paths with the motherfucker. It almost felt like something purposely arranged on a cosmic level, manipulation by the controlling power in the universe, God or whatever the fuck you wanted to call it. He didn't really believe that, though. No way was his role in the scheme of things important enough to warrant divine intervention. This was just one of those times in life when a moment of pure coincidence arrived at just the right time to fuck everything up.

Goddammit.

The part of him that cared about his personal safety above all other things continued to insist there was no real dilemma here. Tyler Barnes was a stranger, one who'd nearly gotten him killed as a consequence of his actions, albeit unintentionally. He didn't owe the guy a goddamn thing, other than maybe sending some karmic payback his way. To do that, all he had to do was get in his car and drive away, let fate sort things out.

Simple and clean. Problem solved.

Except, evidently, his conscience was skittish about actively choosing to do something so callous. Something that, based on everything he knew about the situation, would likely result in Barnes being shot in the head and dumped in the river. Before that, of course, he'd probably be taken to some private location and mercilessly tortured until he surrendered the missing piece of microfilm. In Cole's opinion, the guy was slated for death no matter what. Russell's men would kill him as soon as they had what they wanted.

As he chewed all this over, he found himself wishing he'd issued a quick word of warning while he had the chance. His part of this could be over already. That ship had sailed, however, and now he had a choice to make—tell his conscience to shut up and allow him to slink away like he wanted, or head over to The Gold Rush, find Barnes, and give him an undeserved heads up.

He stared at the other side of the street a moment longer.

Muttering a curse of irritation, he unlocked his car long enough to stow the pistol in the glovebox.

Then he locked the car up again and started walking.

ELEVEN

THERE WAS NO SIGN OF Tyler Barnes anywhere in The Gold Rush. Not in the small bar area one stepped into after coming through the door—a space barely larger than his childhood bedroom—and not in the larger adjacent bar and dining area. Upstairs was an even larger space with a lounge-like vibe. There were low-slung couches, recliners, a few pool tables, and yet another bar.

Barnes wasn't up there either.

Like most every other dive bar Cole had set foot in, the lighting was dim everywhere. The shabby state of the decor might put people off otherwise. He thus took his time searching the place, making sure he was getting a good look at all the patrons, some of whom frowned or gave him nasty looks when they caught him staring. More than once he felt compelled to apologize and explain he thought he recognized someone he'd actually never seen before. He also searched the men's bathrooms upstairs and downstairs. No sign of the slippery motherfucker in those piss-stinking, graffiti-covered shit boxes. That left only the women's restrooms and the kitchen as possible lurking places.

He supposed he could conjure up some reason to slip into the kitchen, but no way in hell would he even consider ducking into the women's bathrooms to check for Barnes. Either some pissed-off chick would claw his eyes out or some dude playing white knight would stomp his ass into the floor for being a creeper. He might even wind up in jail on some trumped-up charge. This didn't seem likely, but he knew from experience things could get out of control fast in situations where alcohol was a factor.

Like this one.

The Gold Rush wasn't too crowded yet and thus far there weren't any obviously belligerent drunks around, so the risk of anything truly crazy happening wasn't huge.

Didn't matter. He wasn't taking the chance.

He went back downstairs and took a seat at the bar in the larger middle area. After removing the mirrored shades and setting them on the bar top, he took a quick glance around. A group of three people were drinking at the end of the bar closest to the entrance and there were more people in one of the booths against the wall behind him. The sound of someone playing the arcade video game in the smaller adjacent bar area was faintly audible, something that wouldn't be possible once the place started to fill up and get noisy.

A slender barmaid in a Bauhaus t-shirt approached and asked him what he wanted to drink. She was pretty, with pale skin and dyed-black hair. He'd seen her here several times going back three or four months, a timeline you didn't have to be Sherlock Holmes to guess most likely coincided with the start of her employment. She never said much, which set her apart from the overly chummy, tip-chasing bar staff he encountered in most places. He figured this was to ward off unwanted romantic overtures. Hard to take that personally.

He started to ask for a Rolling Rock.

Then he remembered the much larger than usual stack of cash in his wallet and ordered a Heineken instead. She gave him a curious look when he handed her a twenty instead of a fiver or his usual assortment of crumpled singles. The look was reflexive surprise, nothing more. She didn't ask about it, moving away after setting a cold green bottle on a napkin in front of him.

He picked up the bottle and took a small first sip.

Sitting down for a beer was pure impulse. His intent upon coming downstairs was to head back across the street, get in his car, and finally get his ass back home. By coming in here to look for Barnes, he'd done his duty as a person in possession of potential life-saving knowledge. No one could say he'd half-assed anything either. He'd checked every nook and cranny of the place to the best of his ability. The guy was gone. Simple as that. What had happened to him after entering The Gold Rush, Cole hadn't a fucking clue. Maybe he'd slipped out a back entrance. Maybe he'd stepped into a magic portal and disappeared into motherfucking Narnia. Cole didn't know and he didn't actually give much of a shit.

All he cared about now was enjoying this frosty, cold beer.

He promised himself he wouldn't linger long, though. There was no guarantee he was out of danger. After all, he'd left behind a pile of dead bodies at the construction site and more of Russell's goons were certain to return to the Elliston Place vicinity at some point.

So he'd just have the one beer and then he'd leave.

He was halfway through that intended one-and-only beer when it occurred to him that removing himself from danger might not be as easy as simply leaving the city. Mr. Russell knew his name. He'd looked at his driver's license, which showed his home address. The man probably hadn't committed the information to memory because, as far as he was concerned, the dopey stoner mistakenly scooped up by his bumbling crew was already dead. After establishing that Cole wasn't who he was after, he likely would've considered anything else about him irrelevant. This line of reasoning made perfect sense to Cole, but it was pure guesswork and he had trouble trusting it.

His paranoia level was just starting to ratchet upward again when his thoughts were interrupted by an abrupt intrusion of loud, discordant music. The amplified needle drop on vinyl startled him slightly. There was a record player behind the bar in the adjacent smaller area, along with an impressive collection of vinyl albums. Sometimes whoever was on duty behind the bar in there would take requests. The last time he was here it was much later at night and the pretty goth bartender who'd served him just now played *Back to Mystery City* by Hanoi Rocks for him after he'd slurred some drunken shit about how much he loved them.

Pretty embarrassing.

He couldn't even remember the girl's name.

Cindy? Cynthia, maybe?

Something like that.

The music playing now was Nirvana. It was "Serve the Servants", the opening song on *In Utero*, the band's latest album. Probably their final album, come to think of it. With everything else he'd been forced to deal with today, he'd almost forgotten about the news of Kurt's death.

The bartender groaned and looked up from the issue of *Propaganda* she'd been reading, her gaze flicking his way. "Well, it's begun. That's all I'll be hearing all fucking night."

Cole was a little taken aback. She'd pointedly directed the comment at him rather than the trio at the end of the bar.

He knocked back a slug of beer. "You don't like Nirvana?"

She shrugged and closed the magazine, placing it on a shelf behind her. "I like *Bleach*."

"The pre-fame album."

She smirked. "Yeah. I know. It's the kind of cooler-than-thou shit posers say. The guys who always claim they liked certain bands better before they signed with a major label."

Cole nodded and affected an exaggeratedly jaded tone. "The Replacements were so much better before they sold out. Those Twin/Tone albums were so raw and real, man. Total punk fucking rock."

She laughed. "Yes! Exactly like that. Only they'd call them The Mats instead of The Replacements."

It was Cole's turn to laugh. "Of course."

She chuckled. "I mean, sometimes they're right, but that doesn't make it any less obnoxious. I really do love *Bleach*, though. The newer stuff is fine, I guess. I've just sort of had my fill of it all."

Cole thought of how often he heard Nirvana's hits on the radio, as well as how the video for "Heart-Shaped Box" had stayed in heavy rotation on MTV for months recently. For a while they'd been on the cover of seemingly every magazine. There was undeniably an overload factor at work and he could understand how some might be sick of them at this point. Same thing had happened with Guns N' Roses a few years earlier.

He sipped his beer again. "I'm not quite at burnout point with them yet, but I get it. You're probably gonna have to listen to people talk about Kurt all night."

She grimaced. "Yeah. Fuck."

The conversation lapsed after that.

Desperate to keep the unexpected moment of interaction going, Cole raised up off the stool long enough to reach into his back pocket and find the Polaroid of Tyler Barnes. "Can I show you something?"

She gave him a wary look. "I guess. So long as it's nothing weird. Don't go creeper on me, dude."

He forced a smile, one he hoped was disarming enough to set her at ease. Maybe he was foolish to think it, but it'd felt like they were connecting in a real way that could either fizzle or turn into something meaningful, depending on what he did next.

"No, it's nothing like that. I was just wondering if you might recognize this guy."

Feeling a bit like a private detective in a movie, he set the photo on the bar and pushed it toward her.

She moved closer and peered down at it.

The change that came over her then was instantaneous and impossible to miss. Her body language became more guarded, and he was able to hear her breathing quicken even over the blaring of the music from the other room. He looked closer and saw her bottom lip quiver ever so slightly as her eyes remained downcast.

Cole frowned. "Something wrong?"

She looked at him then, her eyes radiating an unexpected intensity. "Why are you showing me this? And where did you fucking get it?"

Right away he felt he'd made a mistake. Maybe a big one. One that made him fervently wish he could roll back time a few seconds and leave the picture in his pocket. Showing it to her had seemed a reasonable thing to do. He'd seen Barnes enter The Gold Rush a short while ago. Cole figured maybe she could tell him where he'd gone next. Clearly, though, there was more going on here than met the eye. Maybe this girl and Tyler Barnes knew each other. Maybe Barnes was her boyfriend. And maybe they were both in on whatever scam Barnes was pulling on Mr. Russell. He wanted to think the latter scenario was just his imagination running wild, but he sure as hell wasn't imagining the drastic change in the girl's demeanor.

She was still staring hard at him and now he noticed how her clenched fingers were folding the photograph.

Cole cleared his throat and fumbled for something to say. "Um . . ."

She held up the crumpled photograph and thrust it toward him. "Where did you fucking get this, Cole?"

He gaped at her, stunned that she actually remembered his name.

"Uh . . ." He cleared his throat and felt his face turn hot. The intensity of her glare was making his brain short circuit. "It's kind of a complicated story. I'm not sure how much I should even say."

As much as he liked this girl, the fact was he didn't even really know her. He wasn't so infatuated that he was willing to tell her things that might come back to haunt him. She definitely didn't need to know he'd retrieved the photo from a site where multiple murders had occurred, one of which he'd committed himself. It was too easy to imagine a scenario where the police got involved and she wound up telling them everything she knew. He might have been more loose-lipped with a few more beers in his system, but fortunately half of one Heineken wasn't nearly enough to make him lose all sense of judgment.

She shook her head, sneering in disdain. "Never mind. Wait right there."

Taking the Polaroid with her, she stalked quickly to the far end of the bar, disappearing through a pair of swinging doors into the kitchen.

Cole frowned again and remained where he was, taking another slow sip of Heineken as he eyed those double doors. The kitchen back there mostly only served basic bar food, the starchy kind of stuff that appealed to people when they were three sheets to the wind. Bar staff would sometimes duck back there to do things they weren't supposed to do out in the open, at least not until much later at night, when everyone was too wasted to give a shit about following the rules. At first he figured that was what she was doing. Smoking some weed to settle her nerves. Or maybe doing some coke. Hell, he didn't know her habits.

He drank the rest of his beer and kept glancing back at those double doors, and every single time she failed to reappear.

After a while, one of the guys from the end of the bar approached him. "Hey, man, you know where that chick went? I saw you talking to her. She say she was coming back?"

Cole shrugged. "I guess she sort of implied she was coming back, but I don't really know."

The guy frowned. "What do you mean 'implied'?"

"She said, 'Wait right there,' which I took to mean she'd be back. That's really all I know." Cole gestured at the empty space behind the bar. "But as you can see . . ."

The guy nodded. "Yeah. Maybe we should check the kitchen." He laughed. "Or just help ourselves to some beers. Would serve the lazy bitch right." He cocked his head when he saw Cole frown at his choice of terminology. "No offense, dude. I mean, like, if you're banging her or something."

"I'm not."

The guy laughed and clapped a hand on his shoulder. "Yeah, I didn't think so. She's a little out of your league."

He laughed again and moved away from Cole. In another moment, he saw the guy poke his head through the double doors and start talking to someone in the kitchen. The music and the rising buzz of conversation as more people filtered in from outside made it impossible to hear what was being said from this distance. Side one of *In Utero* was drawing to a close, but even as the music began to fade the conversation remained impervious to eavesdropping.

Seconds later, the guy finally came away from the double doors.

Cole turned on his stool and looked at him. "Find out anything?"

The guy nodded. "Yeah, they're sending someone else out. The bitch took off, man."

TWELVE

SOMEONE ELSE DID COME OUT and start taking drink orders a few minutes later. Cole decided it was time to move on. Tyler Barnes had disappeared and now so had the girl. Unless someone he knew showed up and wanted to hang out, there was no reason to stay. Also, the more he thought about it, the more it seemed like a good idea to avoid this place for a while. Long enough to be reasonably sure any lingering danger related to today's events had passed. A few months should do it. Or so he hoped.

He pushed his stool back from the bar and stood up. Before turning to leave, he retrieved the mirrored shades from the bar top and hooked them over the collar of his new Johnny Cash shirt. He threaded his way through the thickening crowd, pushed through the front door, and stepped out onto the sidewalk, where he moved quickly to the curb. The soundscape of the city was livelier now. More horns honking. More chatter. Laughter. Someone yelling. Briefly heard snippets of music from the open windows of passing cars.

Traffic had slowed considerably and it was easy to weave his way between cars as he hurriedly crossed to the other side of the street. He got his keys out as he stepped into the space between his Tercel and the Ford Taurus next to it. As he opened the Tercel's door and slipped in behind the wheel, he glanced at the music shop and saw a CLOSED sign on the door. He couldn't see inside because the blinds were down.

This was much earlier than he'd expected Sound Stack to close for the night. The clerk in the Mudhoney shirt told him they'd be open until eight. He felt a reflexive twinge of annoyance, thinking of his box of tapes still in there. Then he remembered how he'd been willing to write those off as a loss a little while ago and shrugged. Maybe they'd decided to close early after the news about Cobain. He supposed it was possible. The guy in the Sub Pop shirt had seemed especially upset.

Whatever, man.

He was in the process of leaving already anyway, so what did it matter?

He jabbed the key in the ignition and the Tercel's engine came to life. Beck's "Loser" issued from the speakers at a low volume. The song was starting to feel like his personal theme music. Like Beck himself had peered deep into his soul using some kind of weird hoo-doo magic and then wrote a song about the fucked-up shit he saw. That sense of cosmic fuckery in the timing was present again, just like when he'd crossed paths with Barnes. The song was playing on WKDF rather than on a tape, making the randomness of it extra eerie.

Before he could reach for the gear shifter, a loud tapping on the window made him gasp.

He glanced to his left and felt his guts curdle when he saw a burly man in a black turtleneck sweater pointing a gun at him. His eyes were a piercing blue and he wore his gray hair in a crew cut. He was standing turned to one side in an obvious effort to shield the gun from the view of anyone passing by on the sidewalk.

Cole almost wished the guy would go ahead and shoot him through the window. It was what he deserved for being stupid enough to linger here just long enough for one of Russell's men to catch up to him. That this guy was one of Russell's goons seemed a safe assumption. He guessed it was theoretically possible the guy was a random street thug, but it was unlikely.

The guy tapped on the window harder with the muzzle of the gun. "Get out of the car, punk. People say I've got an itchy trigger finger. Don't make me prove it."

As foolhardy as it seemed on the surface, part of Cole wanted to put this claim to the test. The Tercel's engine was already running. It was highly tempting to put the car in reverse and stomp on the gas pedal. Would the man really turn and start firing as Cole backed recklessly into the street? There were a lot of other people nearby. Potential witnesses and innocent victims, should any stray bullets find unintentional targets. This guy was working hard to project an air of steely resolve and, giving him credit, was doing a damn fine job of it.

But he might be bluffing.

Might be.

Probably was, in fact.

But did Cole really want to risk innocent lives on a hunch?

Shit.

The guy pulled on the door's handle and it came open, making Cole groan as he realized he'd neglected to lock it. Leaning in, the man pressed the muzzle of the gun into his stomach and said, "I can either shoot you where you sit, you little shit, or you can do exactly as I say."

Cole sighed. "I guess I'll do that second thing."

The guy chuckled. "Good choice. Maybe you're not as dumb as I heard." He reached past Cole and took the key out of the ignition, shutting the car off. Then he backed out again, still keeping his back turned to the street. "All right, kid. Get out."

Left with no choice but to acquiesce to the demands of the man who'd probably turn out to be his killer, Cole got out of the car. He closed the door as the man carefully backed off a few steps while keeping the gun aimed at his midsection.

"Are you gonna kill me?"

The guy smirked. "Do you really have to ask?"

He clapped a hand on Cole's shoulder and turned him toward the two-story retail building. The hand stayed there, clamping down hard as he pushed him forward. Twisting out of that grip wouldn't be impossible, but the effort it'd require would remove the surprise factor from any attempt to break free and run for his life.

"Try to run and that'll be it for you, boy," the man told him, as if sensing his thoughts. "Unlike some guys I know, I've got no qualms about shooting a guy in the back."

Cole let out a shuddery breath as they stepped up on the sidewalk outside the line of store fronts. "You'd really do that in front of all these people?"

"Damn right I would." The man's hand moved closer to his neck now, those thick fingers making him grimace as they dug in even harder. "I'd be gone long before any cops could get here. One thing most people are ignorant about is how generally worthless most so-called eyewitnesses really are, especially when you have a bunch in one place like this. They never quite agree on what they saw. You'd be surprised how many times I've gotten away with shooting guys dead in the street."

They arrived at the door to Sound Stack.

"Knock on the door, kid."

"You keep calling me that. I'm not a kid. I'm almost twenty-seven."

"Ah, geeze, I'm sorry I hurt your tender fucking feelings. Some advice for you. You want the real grownups to take you seriously, maybe cut that hippie hair and start dressing like a man instead of a boy." He put the muzzle of the gun against the back of Cole's head. "Now knock on the goddamn door before I blow your fucking brains out."

Cole knocked on the door.

Nothing happened for several seconds. He had time to ponder the significance of why they were now apparently going inside the music shop. Some things started to line up a little in his mind. He'd been snatched off the street shortly after coming out of this place. The kidnappers were looking for Tyler Barnes, who Cole later saw coming at him from the general direction of the shop. He hadn't actually seen him come out through this door, but it seemed a safe bet that's what happened. No way could that be coincidental. It stood to reason Tyler was known to frequent the store around that time, perhaps even on a daily basis, and because he shared a passing similarity to the guy they were really after, his life got fucked up beyond all recognition.

Someone peeled back an edge of the blinds and peeked outside. The thug with the gun moved his head to make his face visible to the person behind the glass. The door opened right away after that and the thug shoved Cole into the music shop.

THIRTEEN

THE PERSON WHO OPENED THE door closed and locked it again once they were inside. First thing Cole noticed was the shop clerks he'd talked to prior to being abducted. Both were alive but appeared to have been roughed up, judging from the multiple facial abrasions and bloody lips. Well, there was another mystery solved. They'd closed up early at the point of a gun, not because they were so shaken by the news about Cobain.

The skinny one in the Sub Pop shirt was on his knees in the middle of the open space between the sales counter and the first row of compact discs. He was weeping and his long reddish-blond hair was hanging over the sides of his face. Blood dripped from his mouth to the floor.

The bigger dude wearing a flannel open over his Mudhoney shirt was on his feet nearby. He wasn't crying, but he was trembling and looked terrified, like someone who knew his remaining time on Earth was likely measured only in minutes at best.

Cole felt terrible for the guy until he remembered he wasn't some casual observer viewing events unconnected to him from some safe distance. Whatever grim fate was about to befall these unfortunate sons of bitches was also coming for him.

Well, this was what he got for trying to be a stand-up guy. A "do the right thing" kind of guy. This was some harsh life lesson shit right here, something he could add to a pile of similar hard lessons he'd failed to properly heed. He reckoned his chances of survival had once again dipped below one percent, but if by some miracle he did live to see another day, he planned to take each and every one of those lessons to heart.

No more trying to be selfless or decent.

No more looking out for anyone other than number fucking one.

Not ever again.

The other thug—the one who'd opened the door—moved into view and Cole felt his gut twist again. It was one of the guys who'd been with Mr. Russell at the construction site. He was a big man and had that same hard look all these men had. Tough with blunt features, sometimes with scars and crooked, oft-broken noses. This one was extra scary because he was the one who'd shot the trench coat-wearing kidnapper. His thick brown hair covered the tops of his ears and made him look like a 50s beatnik compared to his pal with the crew cut.

He looked at Cole and laughed. "Why did you come back here? I'll be honest. I thought no way could you really be as dumb as you seemed when Russell was asking you about the microfiche, but clearly I was wrong. You're even dumber."

Both thugs had a good laugh over that.

Cole shrugged. "I thought I was being careful. Hence the wardrobe change. But I got distracted and didn't clear out of the area soon enough. So, yeah, you're right, I'm pretty fucking dumb." He glanced at the bigger music shop clerk again. "Hey, man, you ever get a chance to look at those tapes?"

The big guy looked briefly confused before recognition dawned in his features. "Oh, hey, you're that guy. The one who was in here when Loder broke the Cobain news on MTV."

Cole nodded. "Yep. That's me."

The clerk gave him a closer once-over. "You look different."

"Things got weird after I left here. So . . . about the tapes?"

The clerk's features took on that faintly sorrowful but resolute cast people in his profession deployed when breaking bad news to customers. "Total I came up with was $23.75. Got a breakdown written up for you. Had to pass on most of that 80s glam shit. That stuff just sits on the shelves. Can't even give it away."

Cole sighed. "I figured. Had to try, though."

"My advice? Just hang onto all that shit until the inevitable nostalgia wave hits. You'll get a much better return."

The thugs listened to this exchange with perplexed expressions, glancing at each other multiple times before the one with the crew cut snapped his fingers in front of Cole's face. "Hey. Fuckhead. Can the music talk. We've got serious business to discuss here."

Cole frowned. "Maybe you have things to talk about with these dudes. I don't know. I'm just an innocent bystander swept up in events beyond my control. You know what else? I still don't even know what the fuck is going on. That's kind of fucked up, don't you think? I'm about to die, probably, based on what Crew Cut said before we came in here, and I don't even know why. That's not cool, man."

The one with the relative abundance of hair started laughing halfway through this speech. "Crew Cut. Holy shit. Who am I to you right now? Hair Guy?"

Cole shook his head. "Right now you're just The Beatnik."

The Beatnik's chuckling gave way to gales of hearty laughter. He started stumbling about the store as his face turned red and the laughter became a physically overwhelming force. Everyone else in the store bore nearly identical expressions of bewilderment. Cole and the clerks even exchanged puzzled looks with the other thug, who kept looking at his partner as if he'd lost his mind.

Crew Cut tried grabbing hold of The Beatnik by an arm to interrupt his fit of maniacal laughter, but the attempt was shrugged away.

"Get a hold of yourself, man!" Crew Cut yelled.

The Beatnik's mania did slowly begin to ebb. He ceased stumbling about and bent over at the waist, putting his hands on his knees as his body continued to quake with a reduced level of laughter. His face was an even deeper shade of scarlet now and he had tears streaming down his cheeks. In Cole's opinion, the man's display of hilarity was wildly out of proportion to the actual level of humor in the remark he'd made. A semi-automatic pistol dangled loosely from the fingers of the man's right hand.

The thin long-haired clerk, still on his knees, looked up through his partial veil of hair and noticed that The Beatnik was standing just a couple feet away. Cole tensed as the clerk—clearly acting on sheer impulse—reached out and tugged the pistol free of the man's grasp.

He then raised the barrel and shot The Beatnik in the face.

Crew Cut screamed in surprise and raised his own weapon, but before he could squeeze the trigger the guy in the Mudhoney shirt barreled into him, hitting the man with enough force to knock him off his feet and send his gun flying. Cole raced after the pistol, scooping it up fast and dancing out of the way as the two larger men rolled around on the floor, clawing, tearing, and biting at each other. There was a moment when it looked like Crew Cut would get the upper hand, but then the clerk got his teeth clamped down on one of the man's ears, growled as he bit through the flesh, and tore away his earlobe.

Crew Cut screamed again, this time in shock and pain.

He kicked and thrashed and finally got free of the clerk, rolling away a couple times before shakily getting to his feet. His eyes were wide with disbelief at the wild and sudden reversal of fortune. Cole understood. He felt much the same way, like he was in some strange dream, the same one he hadn't been able to wake from all afternoon. A long and deranged gangster movie of the mind. *Dumbfellas*. Co-directed by Martin Scorsese, and that new guy Tarantino, while in the midst of an epic bender.

Crew Cut put a shaking hand to his bleeding ear and gaped at them all. His mouth moved and it looked like he wanted to say something, but the words wouldn't come. He looked at the gun barrels pointed his way and made an abrupt decision, turning and running for the door.

The crack of another gunshot made Cole wince as a single bullet drilled into the middle of the man's back, dropping him right as he reached the door.

FOURTEEN

THE THREE OF THEM STOOD there without moving or saying a word for at least thirty seconds, surprised to be alive, their ears still ringing from the gunshots. Three strangers now indelibly united by a shared experience of sudden, bloody violence. There were dead bodies on the floor. Two bad, scary men who by all rights should be on the other side of this equation. A big splash of The Beatnik's blood and brains had hit the sales counter and the wall behind it, with several large globules of brain goo adhering to a Mother Love Bone poster.

Cole heaved a big breath. "Holy motherfucking God." Feeling a strong sense of déjà vu, he took another long look around at the shocking tableau of bloody death before eyeing each of the clerks in turn. "What the fuck now?"

The clerks looked at each other.

Both shrugged.

The big one said, "Dunno, man. Maybe we just hang out and see what happens."

Sub Pop Guy stared at the gun in his hand and frowned. "I think I want to leave." He looked woozy, an impression enhanced by the slight quaver in his voice. "I feel a little sick."

A deep line creased the middle of Cole's brow. "Yeah, I get it. More than you fucking know, trust me. But the gunshots . . . won't the cops be showing up soon?"

The big one's expression turned thoughtful. "Totally possible, but there's also a totally real chance they don't show up at all. In fact, I'd almost be willing to bet they don't."

Cole laughed in a dubious way. "Are you shitting me? Gunshots are, like, serious business, man. And we're not in the hood. 911 is a lot less of a joke this close to the university."

The big one shrugged again. "All true, but think about it. We've been sitting here with our thumbs up our asses for a few minutes already. You hear any sirens yet?"

Everyone went silent a moment.

Cole frowned. "Not yet."

The big clerk nodded. "And what *do* you hear?"

"Ambient noise. Cars. Distant voices. Music from somewhere."

Another nod from the clerk. "Any screaming or other sounds of distress?"

Cole waited another beat and shook his head. "No."

The clerk pointed to the wall to the right of Cole. "The space over there is unoccupied." He did a half turn and pointed to the opposite wall. "Over there is a nail salon run by some chicks who don't like us much. They're already closed for the day, praise Satan." He glanced at the ceiling. "The tattoo parlor directly above us will be open a few more hours yet, but the music you're hearing is that aggro metal they listen to all the time. Prong and Pantera. Helmet. Shit like that."

Cole looked at the ceiling. "Now that you mention it, I do detect a distinct metallic quality to that beat."

The clerk nodded. "Hell yeah, you do. I'm just gonna go ahead and call it. No representatives of the law are en route to this location. Even if someone heard the shots, odds are they don't have clue fucking one where exactly they came from. And all this shit here . . ." He waved a hand at the bodies on the floor. "Well, no one other than us saw it happen."

The thin clerk burped and put a hand to his stomach. "Guys . . . seriously . . . I really think I might—"

He turned away from them and ran to a door at the back of the store. Shortly after disappearing through it, they heard loud retching sounds emanating from some other room.

Cole went to the front door and peeled back an edge of the blinds, peeking outside.

"What do you see?"

The big clerk sounded like he already knew the answer to that question, but Cole told him anyway. "Cars. People walking by on the sidewalk. A drunk guy in a stupid ten-gallon hat hanging onto a parking meter for dear fucking life. He just fell into the street." Carefully avoiding Crew Cut's corpse again, Cole moved away from the door. "No one's paying this place any special attention."

The clerk smiled. "Told ya."

Cole frowned. "Well . . . should *we* call the cops?"

The clerk's smile vanished. He looked taken aback by the suggestion. Shocked, even. "Man. Jesus. Fuck, no. It'd be one thing if they just came racing in like the fucking cavalry, but since that's not happening, we're better off leaving them out of it. You can believe that."

Cole shrugged. "Whatever."

The skinny one groaned as he returned from the bathroom. He looked pale and shaken. There was no sign of the gun he'd used to send two dead goons to their maker. Whether that was by choice or a mere oversight induced by physical distress, Cole did not know, but he could understand if the dude wanted nothing further to do with firearms. He wasn't thrilled to find himself in possession of another one. In fact, now that he had ample firsthand experience with the deadly potential of guns, he felt an intense repulsion for them.

Sub Pop Guy directed a pleading expression at his coworker. "Dude, seriously, for real, I'd like to get the fuck out of here."

The big one nodded and looked at Cole. "Man, I think we're leaving."

Cole grunted. "Which means I've gotta go, too."

Mudhoney Shirt shrugged. "Well, I mean, *yeah*. We can't just leave you here in the shop. Obviously."

Cole nodded and glanced at the front door.

He almost started in that direction but then something massively important occurred to him, something his mind had glossed over in the aftermath of this second heaping helping of psychological trauma. "Hey, wait. Why were those guys beating the shit out of you? Are you friends of that Tyler Barnes motherfucker?"

The clerks traded a wary glance.

Then both sighed heavily.

The big one looked at Cole and said, "You're gonna have to come hang out with us for a bit. This is gonna take some explaining."

FIFTEEN

COLE WENT OUT TO HIS car, got the door open fast, and dropped in behind the wheel. This time he made sure to thumb the lock down the moment the door was shut. He dropped his newly acquired second pistol on the passenger seat, jabbed the key in the ignition, and started the engine.

Getting out of the small parking lot was trickier than it would have been at an earlier hour. There were plenty of people out and about now, much more so than before, with the usual weekend revelry now well and truly underway. He had to back carefully out of the parking space, executing a tight three-point turn to get pointed back toward the street. Then he had to slowly drive up to the sloped edge of the small lot's entrance and wait for a gap in traffic.

It took a while, with a steady stream of foot traffic flowing around the Tercel the entire time. He began to fear he might have to force people out of the way by slowly rolling forward, regardless of whether they were interested in creating room for him. That would be less than ideal. Bumping up against one of these oblivious fools might well result in yet another confrontation with someone interested in hurting him, which was just about the last thing he needed at this point.

Fortunately, that did not prove necessary.

Guiding the Tercel into the tiniest of gaps after several minutes of waiting caused some irritated motorist to lay on their horn in an especially obnoxious manner. In no mood to have his wait prolonged by another several minutes or longer, Cole flapped a hand around in a vaguely apologetic wave and kept going anyway, sighing in relief once his car was finally all the way into the desired lane. Traffic crept along for a bit after that, allowing him to hear a full song and a half on WKDF ("Sex Type Thing" and "Basket Case") before he was at last able to turn down a side street a mere block away from the music shop.

He drove another block down the side street before stopping to flash his lights at the blue Subaru Legacy sedan parked at the corner. The Legacy eased away from the curb. This was all prearranged. The sedan belonged to Zach Nolan, aka Mudhoney Shirt. Also with him was Jeremy Lawson, aka Sub Pop Guy. They were roommates and always rode to work together because Jeremy currently didn't have the funds to fix his inoperable Volkswagen Beetle.

Their intended destination was the apartment complex where they lived, but before reaching the complex, the Legacy pulled into the parking lot of a convenience store. Still tense from his most recent brush with doom, Cole found this deviation from the agreed-upon plan mildly irritating, but he followed the Legacy into the lot.

What else was he gonna do?

The sedan pulled into a spot near the store's entrance and Cole guided his car into the space next to it.

He got out and frowned at the music shop guys as they exited their car. "What's going on? Thought we were headed straight to your place."

Zach threw his door shut and stepped up to the sidewalk. "We decided to get beer. That okay with you, or do you have some kind of moral or philosophical objection to getting utterly shitfaced?"

"I do not."

They went into the store and Cole followed them.

Cole headed straight for the single occupant bathroom in the back. He was behind the closed door long enough to relieve his bladder and have a brief absolute freakout, during which he stared at his reflection in the mirror above the sink and repeatedly mouthed the words *What the fuck?*

After that, he used more of the purloined cash to buy two twelve-packs of Heineken.

Then they left the store and a few minutes later arrived at the apartment complex. It was a big one, with probably at least a dozen and a half buildings—each housing multiple units—spread out over a large piece of land. Cole had lived in a place just like it until recently.

As soon as they were inside the two-bedroom apartment the guys shared, everyone cracked open beers and adjourned to a living room furnished with a recliner, a small sofa, a coffee table, and an entertainment center with a TV and stereo. Stacked many levels high on the table was a pyramid formed from empty Budweiser cans. Sitting near this towering aluminum monument was a black bong in the shape of a skull. Judging from the baked-in musk of the place, the bong likely saw extensive use on any given day. A long row of empty Budweiser cartons lined the tops of the walls all the way around the large room as well as the adjacent dining nook. A model of a majestic sailing ship meticulously crafted from, in large part, sheared slivers of Bud cans was displayed atop the entertainment center. Hanging on the wall behind that was a large Irish flag with a Guinness toucan logo sewn into the middle of it. The whole place was a living shrine to the simple joys of perpetual inebriation.

These were Cole's kind of people.

Their fixation on Budweiser inevitably caused Fear's "More Beer", a rousing ode to relentlessly slamming frosty cold brews, to start running through his head. He wished he had some means of instantly calling up a song to hear in an appropriate moment. That would be so helpful. Alas, his Fear cassettes were in a tape case back home and thus inaccessible for now.

He gulped Heineken and nodded at the beer pyramid. "Impressive."

Zach chuckled. "Indeed. Construction required perhaps two entire days of dedicated drinking. Hard work, but worth it. We're so proud."

Cole gulped more Heineken. "I bet. What would happen if I knocked it over?"

Jeremy snorted from his spot on the opposite end of the sofa from Cole. "We'd have to kill you."

They all laughed.

Zach laughed hardest of all, until his expression abruptly went flat. "But seriously, don't knock it over."

Cole guzzled down the rest of his first beer. "I won't. Not on purpose anyway."

He got up and went into the kitchen to grab another beer.

After reclaiming his previous spot at the end of the sofa, he finally asked the pertinent question. "What the fuck is the deal with Tyler Barnes and what's on that piece of microfilm that's got people so worked up?"

Zach and Jeremy glanced at each other.

Cole groaned in aggravation. "Nope. You're not doing that. No more waffling. No holding back. Tell me everything. Tell me the fucking truth."

Zach frowned. "Honestly, there's some stuff you're probably better off not knowing. I get why you're so worked up, but you don't have anything to do with this business and the best thing you could do is just walk away from it all and never give it another thought."

Jeremy nodded. "He's not lying."

Cole's laughter had a bitter tinge to it. "Here's the thing. My end of this isn't as cut-and-dried as you think. Haven't you wondered why Crew Cut pulled me into your store?"

The roommates exchanged another look.

Zach sipped Budweiser. "Well, now that you mention it . . ."

Cole took another long pull from his second bottle and told them the lurid tale of his abduction and first close encounter with death that day. The way their expressions changed as they listened to his account of events was almost comical, obvious skepticism giving way to wide-eyed astonishment within a span of just a few minutes. Along the way, there were numerous double-takes and more than a few exclamations like, "Oh, man, wow, no fucking way!"

Both gaped at him in goggle-eyed silence for a longish moment when he fell silent.

Then Zach said, "Dude. Holy shit."

Jeremy shook his head. "I can't believe they mistook you for Tyler. That dude's a good half-foot taller than you."

"They weren't very bright."

Jeremy grunted. "Shit. I guess not. Although . . ." A line formed in the middle of his forehead as he pondered the matter a moment longer. "It sounds like these guys never saw Tyler in the flesh before, so maybe they just didn't know about the height thing."

Zach nodded. "Must be the case. These motherfuckers sound like the most underprepared gang of kidnappers in recorded history."

Cole gulped beer. "Based on my experience with them, I'd say that's a more than fair assessment."

Zach shifted in the recliner, making the metal frame beneath the padding squeak slightly. "It's nothing short of goddamn amazing that you made it out of that situation. And then to have things break just the right way to survive a similar thing again a little while later . . . well, it just defies all fucking belief."

Cole cocked an eyebrow at him. "Every word of it is true."

Zach gave his beer can a shake, testing for refill necessity. "Oh, I believe you one-hundred percent. It's just crazy."

Cole's expression turned thoughtful. "I've got this weird karma thing going on today. Bad karma leading into good karma, then back around again and again, like an endless loop I'm trapped in. It's like some *Twilight Zone* shit."

The recliner squeaked again as Zach shifted to the edge of the seat cushion in preparation of standing up. "Dunno, man. I get you're feeling pretty existential right now, which is natural after the scary shit you've been through, but what you're describing isn't really karma as I understand the concept. It's more like just a really weird run of variable luck that against all fucking odds happened to work out your way."

Jeremey laughed. "Like winning the luck lottery."

Zach rose from the recliner and headed for the kitchen. "Exactly like that."

Cole frowned. "What about instant karma?"

Zach guffawed so hard he had to brace a hand against the partition separating the kitchen from the living room to keep from falling over. "That's just a fucking John Lennon song. I don't think it's relevant to your situation." His brow knitted as he spent a few moments mumbling the Lennon lyrics. "Or, shit, maybe it is. In a really, really vague, open interpretation type of way."

"John Lennon was a spy for the CIA," Jeremy put in.

Cole nodded. "Uh-huh. Right. Well, I just really feel like what I've experienced is something more than simple luck. Like, maybe not karma as the swami handbook defines it, but related in a way."

Jeremy said, "Elvis Aaron Presley was also a CIA asset. He was recruited by the organization during his time in the army. The body removed from Graceland in 1977 wasn't really him. His death was faked so he could continue assisting with covert destabilization efforts in South America."

Cole pursed his lips. "Hmm."

Zach returned from the kitchen with a fresh can of Budweiser and dropped back into the recliner. He sipped his new beer and shrugged. "Not saying you're wrong about the karma thing. Doesn't really align with my understanding of how that spiritual mumbo-jumbo shit is supposed to work, but I freely admit I don't speak from a place of real authority."

Jeremy made eye contact with Cole. "What happened after you got away from the kidnapper guys? Did you come straight back to Sound Stack? Because it seemed like you were gone for a while."

Before replying, Cole put his beer down and removed the baseball cap, dropping it on the coffee table. He didn't wear hats as a general rule and now that he was at least temporarily out of danger, it was time to get the damn thing off his head. "No, man, some other shit happened. A little less dramatic, but still weird."

He took his hair out of the ponytail, shaking it out some as he dropped the hair tie on the table.

Then he told them about running into Tyler Barnes outside their shop, along with a detailed account of his fruitless search for the guy inside The Gold Rush. He didn't neglect to tell them about his talk with the goth bartender and her strange reaction to seeing the Polaroid of Tyler.

Zach nodded. "Well, no mystery there. That part of it anyway. The goth chick is Cynthia Rollins. Goes by Cindy. She's Tyler's girlfriend. Probably helped him slip out the back way before you got there. What I don't totally get is why he'd suddenly feel the need to do that."

"Unless he had some hint trouble was coming," Jeremy interjected, staring at the top of his beer can. He lifted his gaze and sipped some beer. "But he seemed fine before that."

"So he was in your shop before I ran into him?"

Zach made an affirmative noise. "Oh, that's another thing. We just work at Sound Stack. Tyler's the boss. The owner of the business. On paper, that is. His dad actually pays the rent and keeps the lights on. Sam Barnes is a rich asshole who has business dealings with that shady-ass Russell motherfucker and *his* boss, Arthur Jamison."

A flicker of excitement stirred in Cole upon hearing that bit of information. Things felt like they might be starting to click into place, like it might finally be possible to start making sense of all the seemingly random weirdness.

He finished his second beer and immediately wanted another one.

Before getting up, however, he asked one more question.

"Tyler stole a piece of microfilm. I know that one basic fact, but nothing else. You guys don't happen to know what makes it so important, do you? I mean . . . what the fuck is on the goddamn thing?"

The question clearly made his hosts uncomfortable. Both fidgeted and shifted around in their seats some more. The silence dragged on long enough to make Cole feel like screaming.

Zach sighed. "Before we get into that, I have a question for you."

Cole shook his head and laughed. "Oh, hell. Why not? Fire away, man."

All trace of humor vanished from Zach's face as he said, "Do you believe in the existence of a world beyond this one?"

SIXTEEN

THESE GUYS SEEMED PRETTY COOL on the surface and Cole was inclined to like them, but already there were worrying indications of some off-kilter beliefs. He considered himself loosely connected to the world of alternative culture and associated leftist philosophies. None of it was anything he thought too deeply about. He didn't spend his spare time reading political essays or attending rallies and meetings. In a general way, though, yes, he saw himself as being on that side of things, and he liked to believe he had an open mind about a lot of stuff.

To his way of thinking, however, there was a massive difference between rational non-mainstream ideas and believing that dead rock stars led double lives as CIA spooks. And now this question about a world beyond this one. A question that, if posed by anyone else, would almost certainly be followed up with some tiresome Jesus saves crap, but these guys weren't cut from that cloth. No, whatever Zach was getting at here would likely be something far loonier. He gave brief consideration to simply getting up and walking out but quickly discarded the idea. These guys still represented his best hope of making sense of things, so he at least needed to see where this was going.

He let out a long sigh and shook his empty bottle, thinking about how much he wanted another one.

But first . . .

"What do you mean by that? Like, as in an afterlife?"

Zach shook his head. "No, of course not. That's a mystery none of us will know the answer to until after we pass on. I'm talking about actual other worlds, other planets and mortal realms on different planes of existence."

Cole squinted. "Uh-huh. Okay, I can already tell I'm gonna need to piss and grab another beer before continuing this conversation. Mind if I avail myself of the facilities?"

Zach laughed. "You think we're crazy, don't you?"

"I don't know what I think yet."

Zach nodded, chuckling again. "Fair enough." He pointed to an archway to the right of the entertainment center. "Bathroom's down the hall there."

Cole got up and headed that way without another word, locking himself in the bathroom and turning the fan on prior to taking a piss. A *Sid and Nancy* movie poster was thumb-tacked to the wall above the toilet tank. It was frayed at the edges and there were bits of yellowed tape at the corners from when it'd previously been attached to some other wall. He looked at the smirking face of Gary Oldman, the actor who played Sid Vicious in the movie, and felt a strange tingling at the back of his neck. There were signs and portents of potentially momentous things everywhere if you were paying attention.

Just a few minutes ago, Jeremy was invoking the names of dead rock and rollers in connection to shadowy, sinister things. It was all nonsense, in Cole's opinion. Except now here was a representation of yet another dead rocker staring him in the face in what he was just buzzed enough to see as a mocking way. And all this on the day the death of the latest true rock icon was announced to the world. All of it was coincidental and probably signified nothing. He'd been through some weird shit and now his trauma-addled brain was seeing patterns in random things. These Sound Stack guys weren't normal. They were hardcore music nerds. You couldn't reasonably expect to spend any significant time inside the abode of such people without the subject of dead musicians coming up.

There was nothing more to it than that.

Probably.

As his urine stream slowed to a trickle, Cole glanced over at a basket on the floor near the toilet. It was filled with magazines. On top was an old, well-worn copy of *Rolling Stone* with Jim Morrison on the cover.

"Jesus fucking Christ."

Cole zipped up and washed his hands.

Then he left the bathroom, grabbed another bottle of Heineken from the fridge, and again returned to his previous spot on the sofa.

He immediately picked up on a subtle shift in the vibe of the room. A large purple candle in a glass jar had materialized from somewhere, already giving off a pungent scent he could not identify. It was on the coffee table near the skull bong. The candle was the only visible evidence of the change Cole sensed, but he knew there was more to it than that. Something felt off about the music shop guys, too, though outwardly they looked the same. He was at an utter loss to explain it for a span of nearly half a minute.

Then he had an inkling of a suspicion.

"What fucking drugs are you guys on now?"

Zach's laugh was the loudest such sound he'd produced in Cole's presence thus far. "A powerful hallucinogen that will take full effect in roughly thirty minutes."

A corner of Cole's mouth curled slowly upward in a despairing sneer as he took a moment to look each of them in the eye. "Both of you did this?"

They nodded.

"Oh, hey," Zach said, frowning now. "I'm sorry, man, we've been rude. Do you want to trip with us? We've got more acid. Some magic mushrooms too, if that's your preference."

Cole shook his head. "Thanks, but no. And why the fuck would you do this? Why now?"

The roommates glanced at each other and shrugged.

Zach said, "Just seemed like the thing to do at the end of a stressful day."

"And I thought it might help me come to peace with my new reality as a killer of men," Jeremy added. "Good acid has spiritual healing properties."

"I see. And what's up with the candle?"

Zach frowned. "Dude. We're burning it in honor of Kurt. Like a vigil sort of thing. Oh, shit. We should put on some music."

The tortured metal frame of the old recliner squeaked again as he heaved himself up and went to the stereo. Some lights came to life on the various components as he pressed a button. He opened a cabinet beneath the CD player and grunted as he knelt to examine the large selection of discs stored there.

Cole scowled. "Man, come on, we don't have time for this. I've barely gotten any real answers out of you fuckers, and now according to you I've got less than half an hour before you're basically useless."

"Hold on. This will only take a minute. Not even that."

True to his word, Zach was back on his feet seconds later. He opened a compact disc case, hit a button to open the CD player's tray, and inserted the disc. Another button tap closed the tray and yet another one started the music. Heavy bass notes signaled the beginning of "Blew", the lead track on *Bleach*.

Zach bobbed his head in time to the music for a moment before dropping back into the recliner.

He looked at Cole and said something indecipherable over the blaring music.

Cole got up and went to the stereo, twirling the volume knob until it was at a level conducive to conversation.

He returned to the sofa and glared at Zach. "If I didn't know any better, I'd think you guys were purposely trying to avoid telling me something. I'm done putting up with it. So here it is. I don't know if I believe in the existence of a world or worlds beyond this one. I need you to go ahead and tell me what the fuck that has to do with whatever the fuck is on that piece of microfilm. Like, completely stop fucking around and just tell me. Now. Pretty please."

The roommates exchanged yet another wary glance.

Then Zach sighed and said, "It wasn't just one piece of microfilm he stole, though one is all he has left at this point. We know there were many more because we saw them. They showed stolen documents and photographic evidence of many strange things, including the truth behind some of history's greatest mysteries. Information various governments and organizations would like to keep secret. There are images of strange artifacts and corpses of beings from other worlds. What those in the know refer to as 'visitors'."

"Aliens," Jeremy added, nodding along. "That's what he means."

Cole gave him a squinting sidelong glance. "Yeah, I figured that out, thanks." His gaze settled on Zach again. "You say these mystery documents and whatnot were stolen. From where?"

Zach guzzled beer and resumed bobbing his head to the beat of the music. "From a secret vault beneath the Vatican. A vast repository of all the world's most arcane knowledge. Only a few living souls have ever seen any of it."

Cole laughed. "And yet somehow proof of this rare, secret knowledge wound up in the possession of Tyler fucking Barnes? An ordinary, everyday douche? How is that possible?"

"Well, he was never in possession of the actual documents or artifacts. Just microfilm. The theft of the actual stuff was accomplished by mysterious motherfuckers operating at a much higher and way more serious level of criminal enterprise."

Cole leaned back on the sofa and took a long, contemplative pull from his latest Heineken. "So . . . that's all there is then? Some pictures and documents? Stuff that for all anyone knows is fake?"

Zach's heavy sigh suggested he was growing weary of his guest's skepticism. "I know it sounds off-the-wall, but trust me, it's all real. And, no, that's not all there is to it. What's truly dangerous about the microfilm is that it's a tangible link to one of the most brazen acts of thievery committed in modern times. There's a literal army of spies and assassins searching the globe for the trove of priceless shit that was stolen. Serious motherfuckers willing and authorized to do whatever it takes to get it all back. And if for any reason you wind up on their radar, well, you might as well find yourself a shotgun and do what Kurt did, because that'd be less painful than whatever those jackbooted fuckers would put you through."

Maintaining a blank expression as he listened to Zach's speech—which to Cole sounded little different from the unhinged ravings typical of homeless schizophrenics he sometimes encountered in the city—was not easy. The corners of his mouth kept twitching and it was frequently necessary to bite down hard on his bottom lip, but somehow he managed to keep a lid on his true feelings long enough to hear the guy out.

"That's very interesting," he said at last, following yet another thoughtful silence. "Assuming all this is true, how did Tyler get involved?"

Zach took a swig of beer. "Remember what I told you about his father being a rich asshole?"

Cole nodded. "Yeah."

"Well, rich assholes are like the rest of us in one important way," Zach said. "They socialize primarily with people of a similar background and social stature. *Other* rich assholes, in other words. This Russell person you talked to, he's one of them, but he's a peasant compared to Tyler's dad. And Tyler's dad is a peasant compared to

Arthur Jamison."

Cole frowned. "Are you saying Jamison himself is connected to the Vatican theft?"

Zach pointed a finger at him and said, "Bingo. Bankrolled the whole thing. We know this because the proof is on the remaining piece of microfilm Tyler still has. Tyler went with his dad to some swanky party at Jamison's penthouse downtown. It was supposed to be an indoctrination of sorts. Sam Barnes wanted his kid to make connections, start forming relationships with the right people. Anyway, the way he tells it, he got drunk as shit and went exploring, then happened to wander by the wrong door and overheard some strange shit. Gross rich guys gossiping over cigars and scotch, tongues getting a little looser than they should. He did some more exploring and wound up in Jamison's home office. And that's where he found it, the file filled with hundreds of pieces of microfilm. A cornucopia of incriminating shit. It was open right there on Jamison's desk. Or so he says."

"And you believe him?"

Zach shrugged. "Maybe it didn't happen *exactly* the way he says, but I think it's pretty close. You're right about him being kind of a jerk, but he's not really as stupid as you think. His judgment was impaired and he did a dumb fucking thing. He grabbed the folder and slipped out of there."

Cole frowned. "And he told you guys about all this for what reason?"

The big guy's facial muscles contorted in a strange way and then he looked up at the ceiling, peering intently at a thin crack in the plaster for a moment before again looking at Cole. "He brought the file here because I have a microfilm reader."

"Why the fuck do you have a microfilm reader? Were you a librarian in a past life?"

Zach sighed. "It's not that weird a thing, man. My granddad was a newspaper reporter and he had one for home use. I inherited all his shit after he passed. A lot of it I donated or junked, but some I kept, including the reader. I thought it was neat. If you don't believe me, go peek in my bedroom. It's right there on my desk. Anyway, Tyler knew about it and asked to use it. At that point I had no idea what we were getting into and didn't think it was a big deal. Then we spent hours poring over all that stuff. By dawn, we were pretty freaked out about it."

Not rolling his eyes required another conscious effort of will. "How high were you that night?"

Zach scowled at the insinuation. "Not nearly high enough to imagine any of what we saw. Jeremy can vouch for that."

"Damn right," the largely silent roommate confirmed.

"And how long ago was this?"

The roommates looked at each other.

Zach shrugged. "Six or seven days ago, I think. May have lost a day there the last time we tripped, which was the day after, but I think that's right."

"So what happened then? How did Jamison know who took the file?"

Zach grunted. "A combination of simple deduction and bad luck. Tyler left without telling anybody. If he'd come on his own, maybe it wouldn't have mattered, but he rode there with his dad, so his disappearance was immediately deemed suspicious. Tyler was already in hiding by the time the theft was noticed. A few days later he had someone drop off the bulk of the file at his father's office. But he did one last dumb thing."

"He kept a piece of microfilm. The most dangerous one of all."

Zach's beer can slipped from his fingers and hit the carpeted floor. He gave no indication of noticing. "That's true, buckaroo."

Jeremy giggled.

Zach slumped down in the recliner. "He didn't think anyone would notice that just one was missing. Dude was fucking wrong."

He slumped down even further.

Cole drained the last of his beer. "And today he visited Sound Stack. Why? Did he have reason to think he was safe again?"

Zach's mouth dropped open but no words emerged as he resumed staring at the crack in the ceiling.

Jeremy's head swiveled slowly in Cole's direction. "He did think he was almost in the clear. Wouldn't say why, but he did seem to believe it. I think he was deceived."

Cole nodded. "Lured out into the open somehow?"

"Yeah."

Jeremy got up and went into the kitchen, disappearing from sight as soon as he was behind the waist-high partition. One second he was there, the next he was gone. Cole spent some moments gripped by intense paranoia, a shift in perception fueled by the many strange if improbable things he'd been told tonight. He briefly believed the guy had vanished into thin air, perhaps slipping through some crack in reality into another world.

Then he heard the quiet sobbing.

Cole got up and went into the kitchen.

Jeremy was on the floor, lying on his side in a fetal curl.

Cole shook his head. "Fuck this."

He stepped around the distraught music shop clerk, opened the refrigerator, and removed the rest of his beer. There was still a lot of it left. Still a lot of the night left, for that matter, and he didn't want to waste another second of it in the company of these loons. He still figured he'd like them under normal circumstances, but that description decidedly did not apply to this evening.

Leaving the apartment's front door unlocked, he carried the Heineken twelve-packs down to his car. After stowing them in the back, he returned to the apartment to find nothing had changed. Zach was still staring slack-jawed at the ceiling and Jeremy was still weeping quietly out of sight in the kitchen. He passed through the living room and walked down the hallway until he found what he guessed was Zach's bedroom. There was a desk near the bed. The microfilm reader was right where Zach said it would be.

Cole grunted. "Huh."

After taking another piss, he returned to the living room and tried to talk to Zach. "Any idea where I might find Tyler tonight? Or Cindy?"

Zach said nothing.

A faint voice drifted in from the kitchen: "Try the Hydra."

Cole frowned. "What is the . . . oh, wait. That weird nightclub over on the east side?"

"Yeah . . . dude."

"Thanks for the tip."

A sniffle. "No prob."

On his way out of the apartment, Cole paused long enough to sweep a hand through the middle of the towering beer can pyramid. The tinkling sound of empty aluminum cans hitting the coffee table and rolling to the floor made him smile as he walked out the door.

SEVENTEEN

COLE TURNED DOWN WINSTON AVENUE, a lonely two-lane side road on the east side of the city. He passed empty lots where concrete slabs with weeds growing up through cracks were the only remnants of recently razed old buildings. The first standing building he saw was two blocks up the street, a shuttered old gas station with plywood over the windows and a lot of prominent NO TRESPASSING signage. Another block up were two active places of business, a beer store and a porn shop facing each other from opposite sides of the street.

Coming up on the right, at the far end of the street, was the Hydra. He pulled into the parking lot and guided the Tercel into a vacant space at the end of the back row. More open spaces in the rows in front of him allowed for a decent view of the club's entrance.

He was familiar with the area from visiting the club in its former incarnation as a conventional strip club. The place was still an "adult" entertainment venue, or so he'd heard, but not the kind that attracted a mainstream crowd. Strange stories sometimes circulated about the Hydra, including that it was "fetish friendly" and that there were rooms that functioned as dungeons. It was said to be extremely popular with the whips and chains crowd. Some even said occult ceremonies took place down in the basement. Maybe even human sacrifices.

Cole had no firsthand knowledge of any of that. He hadn't been inside the building since the change in management. No one he knew had ever voiced any desire to check the new place out. His friends were a largely conservative lot when you really got down to it. The mere prospect of circulating among genuine freaks and kinksters made them feel uptight. Cole did not exclude himself from this assessment. He'd never seriously considered visiting the Hydra, despite harboring a more than mild level of curiosity.

Even now he felt a deep apprehension.

Normally, in any situation even remotely similar, it was the company of friends that gave him the courage necessary to go through with things that made him nervous, but that wasn't an option this time. He felt frozen behind the wheel of the Tercel, mired in a state of hopeless indecision.

He wound up spending the next twenty-odd minutes sipping a Heineken and staring at the club's entrance. The building's outward appearance was drastically different from what he remembered. Gone were the giant neon signs alerting passing motorists to the presence of "the hottest naked girls in town." The building's exterior was now a solid monolithic black instead of pink and purple. Above the entrance was a sign showing a painted image of a Hydra, the many-headed serpent of myth. No name was displayed, but Cole supposed it wasn't really necessary. A place like this thrived on reputation and word-of-mouth rather than traditional advertising.

He finished off his beer and tossed the empty bottle in the back. The additional influx of alcohol had not helped him arrive at a decision. He sat up straighter behind the wheel and spent some moments trying hard to psych himself up to go do what he'd come here to do. In his mind, he saw himself exit the car and walk fast toward the entrance, but in reality his legs still felt like they were made of cement. The internal debate made him feel like an unsophisticated loser, more like the small-town kid he still was at heart than a worldly adult.

"Goddammit."

He couldn't stay here like this much longer.

Sooner or later, someone would take note of him and become suspicious, maybe even think he was up to something shady. Maybe even call the police on him, which was basically the exact last fucking thing he needed at this particular juncture in his life.

Whatever. Stop being a pussy. Fucking do this.

Cole got out of the Tercel and slammed the door shut. He sucked in a big breath of cool evening air, feeling his heart race.

Then he started walking.

EIGHTEEN

A BURLY BEARDED GUY WITH an abundance of tattoos and an unusual number of facial piercings asked to see his ID. With his shaved head and all the steel embedded in his face, he looked like he could be one of the Cenobites in *Hellraiser*. Cole opted to keep this observation to himself, figuring it'd make him look like the hopeless rube he in actual fact was.

He took out his wallet and showed the man his driver's license. The guy looked it over and handed it back. "There's a ten-dollar cover charge."

Cole opened the wallet, took out a twenty, and handed it over.

The man dragged a wad of cash out of a hip pocket, peeled back some bills until he found a ten-note, and gave it to Cole. Then he cocked one of his pierced eyebrows. "Been drinking, eh?"

"Um . . ."

The man laughed. "I'm not a fucking cop. I don't care how much you drink, as long as you behave." He gave Cole a quizzical look. "You plan on behaving, Johnny?"

Being referred to by this name confused Cole until he realized it was a reference to the face adorning his new shirt. He nodded. "Absolutely. I'm not a troublemaker."

"Good to hear. I'd hate to have to toss you out on your ass."

Cole allowed the Cenobite-looking dude to stamp the back of his hand. The blurry stamped image vaguely resembled a skull. At that point he was allowed to proceed down a short hallway and into the main part of the club.

The layout of the place remained much as he remembered from the days when rowdy regulars turned up in droves to ogle tits and ass, the dancers shaking it to the sleazy strains of "Cat Scratch Fever", "Girls, Girls, Girls", and the like, but the general vibe was immensely different now. There were tables and booths, and a stage with a runway in front. Those things were the same as before, but the lighting was much dimmer these days, effectively hiding the faces of the people seated in the booths along the walls. There was a girl up on the stage, but instead of strutting up and down the runway and striking overtly sexual poses, she was swaying slowly to the hypnotic beat of Christian Death's "This Is Heresy." She stood in six-inch platform heels at the edge of the runway with her back turned to the audience, her slender, pale form almost entirely exposed save for the shiny black panties he figured were either latex or leather.

Some aspects of what he was seeing and hearing more or less matched what he'd imagined, but the atmosphere was more subdued than he'd expected. Instead of wading into a churning mass of leather and latex-clad humanity going wild to the industrial sounds of Skinny Puppy or Ministry, he found himself in the midst of what could charitably be described as a sparse crowd. The shadowy booths looked close to full, but only maybe half the tables had people sitting at them. No one other than the girl on stage was dancing, and the music was playing at a moderate volume allowing for conversation.

A few more people were seated on stools at the bar. Cole did a double-take when he saw the bartender. For a moment he was certain he'd found Cindy, but then he realized it was someone who sort of looked like her from a distance, with the same ghostly pale skin and dyed-black hair. The shape of her body was distinctly feminine beneath her tight shirt and black jeans, but she had broader shoulders and a build that made her look like she worked out a lot. She was also taller than Cindy by at least several inches. This was disappointing, but the woman might be a good first person to approach with his questions about Cindy and Tyler. Talking to a bartender, after all, would be less awkward than walking up to random patrons.

Before he could approach the bar, something made him turn back toward the stage. The dancer was facing the crowd now. Pasties with tassels covered her otherwise bare breasts. A man operating a video camera stood near the stage, with the camera aimed at the end of the runway. A black mask hid the top half of the dancer's face. She was still swaying in that almost drugged way as the song neared its conclusion.

At the same time, a man in a black suit and tie approached her from behind. He was older, with slicked-back gray hair and age spots on his weathered face. In his right hand was a revolver. He came to a stop directly behind the swaying woman, raised the gun, and aimed it at the back of her head.

Cole tensed and said, "Wait."

No one heard him because in that same instant there was a loud bang from the gun. The dancer dropped to her knees at the edge of the stage, and after another moment, toppled over onto her side. The man with the gun turned away from her and walked back down the runway at an unhurried pace, soon disappearing behind the curtain at the back. Cole felt on the verge of hysterics until he realized no one else in the club seemed the least bit concerned. They sat at their tables in nonchalant poses, nursing cocktails and smoking cigarettes as they engaged in quiet conversation.

Two men in basic custodial garb came out and took hold of the "dead" woman's ankles. They started dragging her limp form toward the back of the stage. Another song began issuing from the speakers before they could get her out of sight, "Garbageman" by The Cramps. Cole wondered if the song choice was someone's idea of a twisted joke, a sick interpretation of what the men on the stage were doing. *Taking out the garbage.*

The word "dead" existed in quotes in his head because he was sure what he'd just seen was some form of playacting or performance art. A modern day Grand Guignol kind of thing, maybe. It was the only way the non-reaction of the jaded crowd made any sense. It would also explain the brief presence of the camera operator, who'd disappeared in the wake of the fake shooting. "Alternative" this place might be, but they weren't going to murder someone right out in the open.

Right?

Right.

He went to the bar and leaned against it instead of sitting on a stool. The bartender chick took a moment to notice him and when she did the cast of her features changed, conveying open disdain. He was a little hurt by that. Sure, he didn't much resemble the rest of the clientele, many of whom had what he thought of as that hip New York or Paris art crowd look. That disaffected and drug-damaged but somehow still effortlessly glamorous look. These simply weren't his people, if he was being honest with himself, but he'd imagined he might nonetheless come off as cool enough to hang with them anyway.

Apparently not.

With grudging reluctance, the bartender finally made her way over to him. "What do you want?"

Slightly strange way to phrase that, but he shrugged. "Um . . . a beer?"

"What kind?"

She said it like he was stupid, in a deeply condescending tone.

"Heineken."

"Okay."

Even more disdain than before. It was almost impressive how little she gave a shit about living up to the basic standards of good customer service. She grabbed a Heineken from the fridge behind the bar, opened it, and set it on a napkin in front of him.

He dropped some bills on the bar and said, "That wasn't real, was it? That, uh, incident on the stage. It was all an act."

She shrugged. "Who's to say? Reality is subjective."

Cole knocked back some beer. "Right, whatever, but I know what I saw. There was no exit wound. No splash of blood. The real thing is a lot messier than what happened up there. Believe me, I know. I bet that was a blank round the old dude fired."

The bartender stared blankly at him. "Believe what you want. Choose your own reality. I have nothing else to say about it."

The steely resoluteness in her tone made him realize it was time to move on. "That bullshit was about as convincing as a junior high play, but okay. I actually need to ask you about something else."

"Hitting on me is a waste of your time."

Cole laughed. "No shit. Already figured that out. I was told I might find some friends of mine here."

The bartender smirked. "I find that hard to believe."

"What, that I'd know the kind of people who hang out here?"

She shook her head. "I find it hard to believe you'd have friends at all. You're loathsome. The human equivalent of a grub worm."

Cole grunted. "I see. Well, the people I'm looking for are Cindy Rollins and Tyler Barnes. You know them?"

Her smirk vanished. "Hold on."

She turned away from him and went to a phone mounted on the wall behind the bar, lifting the receiver off the hook and putting it to her ear. Her index finger stabbed a single button on the number pad. She was partly turned away from him and her voice was inaudible below the music, but he caught a glimpse of her lips moving. The call lasted only a few seconds.

Her face was blank again as she came back and said, "Wait right here."

He started to tell her he wasn't going anywhere, but she was already moving away from him. She returned to her previous position at the opposite end of the bar and engaged in quiet conversation with the people seated there. A chic-looking young woman with hair cut in the style of a 1920s flapper girl looked over at him, gave him a blatant once-over, sneering in disgust before turning away from him.

Cole frowned.

Jesus fucking Christ.

Next time he went out on his own he'd just go to Hooters. At least the girls there would pretend to like you long enough to take your money.

He put his back to the bar and stared at the stage, gulping more beer as he waited to see if the club would trot out any kind of follow-up act. None materialized in the time he spent standing there, but he did continue to enjoy the music selections. He heard "Funtime" by Iggy Pop and "Wait for the Blackout" by The Damned. Almost everything played since he'd stepped through the front door was something he liked, an irony that made the harsh reception go down even more bitterly. It wasn't fun being scorned by those whose approval he'd love to have.

The sudden intrusion of a gruff voice made him flinch. "Young man."

Cole looked to his left and felt his heart flutter when he saw the older man who'd fired the revolver at the back of the dancer's head. He gripped the Heineken bottle tighter to keep it from slipping out of his fingers. "You talking to me?"

The old guy began turning away from him. "This way, please."

Cole shrugged.

He followed the man around the tables and then down a hallway to the right of the stage. In the hallway, they passed a couple of closed doors before arriving at an open one at the end of the passage.

The old guy stood outside the door and motioned for Cole to enter with a wave of his hand.

Cole peeked inside and saw a small managerial office with a dinged-up old metal desk that took up most of the room. Behind the desk was a swivel chair and in front of it was a cheap-looking metal folding chair for guests or subservients. Against the wall to the left of the desk was a small filing cabinet. Directly opposite the front of the desk was a closed door to what he assumed was a closet. And that was it. No framed photos, wall decorations, or anything else in the way of personalization. All in all, a pretty bleak space.

"No one's in there."

The old guy nodded. "Go on in and have a seat."

Cole entered the office and glanced back at the old man, who was already beginning to close the door. "Oh, hey. Nice performance out there. Is it weird pretending to kill someone in front of an audience?"

No reply.

The door closed.

An instant later, he heard a rattle from inside the doorknob. He went to the door, gripped the knob, and tried to turn it. It rattled slightly, but would not turn.

Locked from the outside.

Cole gulped. "Uh-oh."

NINETEEN

COLE SET THE NOW EMPTY Heineken bottle on the desk and returned to the door, trying it again. This time he gripped the door-knob with both hands and exerted a great deal more pressure, but the result was the same. The knob barely budged. He stepped back and studied the door and frame more closely. His pulse was racing and he was right on the edge of being truly afraid again, but the door didn't look especially solid. The wood looked old to his eyes. That, along with the slight rattle the knob made when he shook it, led him to believe he could probably kick or batter his way through the thing.

That he might even need to attempt such a thing blew his fucking mind. Yes, he'd been nervous about entering the Hydra, but at no point prior to stepping through that front door had he thought he'd be running into any real trouble. At worst, if some of the rumors about the place turned out to be true, he thought he might endure some moments of severe embarrassment. Instead, he'd stumbled into yet another dicey situation. He was starting to feel like a glutton for punishment, or perhaps just a garden variety fool who didn't know any better than to not keep sticking his nose where it didn't belong.

He could be in his room at his parents' house right now, quietly enjoying a few more beers while watching *Basket Case* or *The Toxic*

Avenger for the umpteenth time. It was how he'd been spending most nights lately after losing the latest job. Being back with the parental units wasn't ideal for a wide range of reasons, but at least it always felt safe.

A rattle again came from inside the doorknob while he was still in the midst of questioning the many dubious choices he'd made not only that evening but throughout his entire wasted life so far. He took an unconscious step backward as the door began to swing inward.

Then Cindy Rollins was standing there in the open doorway, frowning as she peered in at him. "You again."

Not exactly the warmest of greetings.

Even after all the weird shit that had happened, it was a bit off-putting. There was no reason for her to greet him like some long-lost old friend, of course. They still barely knew each other. Given the overall friendly nature of their previous interaction, however, her attitude toward him was a disappointment. All of which he was barely able to start processing before considering how odd it was to see her out there in the hallway. She was alone as far as he could tell, with no threatening presence lurking nearby.

Cole nodded. "Yeah. Me again."

She came into the office, dropping the key she'd used to unlock the door on the desk as she settled into the chair behind it. After propping her feet on a corner of the desk, she interlaced her fingers and looked up at him. "I hear you were looking for me. Well, here I am. What do you want?"

Cole frowned. "You look weirdly comfortable behind that desk."

"There's nothing weird about it. It's my fucking office."

Cole scratched his chin. "That's . . . interesting. The list of things I don't understand just keeps getting longer."

"My guess is that was a long list even before today." She indicated the other chair with a tilt of her chin. "If you want some things cleared up, have a seat and I'll tell you what I can, which might not be much."

Cole sat opposite her after a brief hesitation. "So . . . this is your club?"

She shrugged. "I'm the manager. I don't own the place."

"But you work at The Gold Rush."

She nodded. "That's right. I have two jobs, like lots of other people. Nothing mysterious about that. Or do you generally have a hard time grasping basic shit?"

Cole grunted. "Where's Tyler?"

"He's not here. And I'm not comfortable discussing my boyfriend with a dude who, for all I know, is some kind of obsessed stalker."

Once again, Cole was taken aback by her attitude. He sputtered for a moment or two before managing to get out a coherent response. "I'm not a stalker. Jesus. That's . . . well, it's ridiculous."

She gave him a dubious look as she watched him shift around on the chair. "Is it, though? Look at it through my eyes. You always try to talk to me at The Gold Rush. Oh, yeah, I know, you try to play it cool, but you're always watching me. And now you've tracked me down to my other job. A job I've never told you about. What other fucking way am I supposed to take that?"

A deep furrow formed in the middle of Cole's brow as he squirmed on the edge of the chair. "Okay, well . . . shit, I'm sorry. I hadn't thought about it like that. I can see your point, but I swear I'm not up to anything creepy. Today has been a really weird fucking day. I'm not even kidding. I have reason to think Tyler might be in trouble, and, uh . . ."

She squinted at him. "What the fuck is your deal? I'm sure that's not the most comfortable chair in the world, but you're squirming around like a dude sitting on a bed of hot fucking coals."

He grimaced. "I'm starting to realize how badly I have to piss. I've, uh, had several beers."

"No shit." She lifted her chin again. "My private bathroom is right behind you. You can use it if you promise not to spray piss everywhere."

"I wouldn't."

"Just hurry up."

He went into the bathroom and shut the door behind him. The bathroom was clean but tiny, not much larger than a small closet. There was no fan, so to avoid making an embarrassingly loud splattering sound, he angled his urine stream so it hit the inside of the toilet bowl above the water level. Maintaining this in a way that didn't result in a mess required a significant level of concentration. The effort made him realize how close he was to being actually drunk instead of just buzzed. He wasn't quite there yet, which felt important. Cindy was disorienting him with her responses thus far, making him feel even more foolish than usual. He couldn't allow that to make him lose sight of his many valid concerns.

Cindy was using the desk phone as he came back out into the office. She was still leaning back in her chair, talking softly to someone with the receiver balanced between her shoulder and chin.

Still addressing whoever was on the other end, she chuckled and said, "Appreciate it." The base of the phone sat at the edge of the desk. She returned the receiver to the cradle and looked at him. "Feel better?"

He sat again. "Yeah, thanks."

She nodded. "You were saying something about Tyler being in trouble. Why would you think that?"

Cole glanced again at the room's open hallway door. Then he gave her the best no-nonsense look he could manage. "I'll get into that in a second, but maybe you could tell me something first. Why did that old guy lock me in here?"

"You weren't locked in here."

Cole looked at the key on the desk. The same one she'd used to unlock the door maybe ten minutes earlier.

"Huh. You know what? I think I'm gonna leave."

The little smile that formed at the edges of her mouth was a touch disturbing. "But you haven't told me why you think Tyler's in trouble. If you weren't lying about that, I should know. I wouldn't want anything bad to happen to him."

Cole began to rise up out of his chair.

In the same instant, the bartender who'd treated him with such withering disdain came through the door bearing two fresh bottles of Heineken. Both already had the caps removed. She offered one to Cole, who accepted it after a brief hesitation and sat back down, discombobulated by the arrival of apparently free beer. Never mind that there was still plenty of Heineken out in his car. There was a principle at stake here. Rejecting an offering of beer with no accompanying expectation of payment was the kind of bad karma thing that could set the universe out of alignment. Or maybe not, but he thought he should probably err on the side of caution in such matters.

After setting the other bottle near the edge of the desk, the bartender turned to leave, but stopped when Cindy said, "Could you stay for a bit, Nikki? Cole has some important information to share and maybe some things he'd like to get off his chest. I think it'd be good to have an impartial observer present."

Nikki smiled. "No problem."

She went to the hallway door and closed it.

Cole's heart rate spiked as Nikki then took up a position directly behind him. He'd known she was one of the taller women he'd ever met during his time talking to her from the other side of a bar, but it was something he hadn't fully appreciated until just now, with the way she was looming over him. He guessed she was an inch or two over six feet, an estimation he supposed might be slightly off, but likely not by much. He was shorter than her by several inches no matter what.

He again started to rise from the chair. "I really think I've changed my mind about all this."

Nikki put her hands on his shoulders and firmly pushed him back down. Her hands did not retreat once his ass was touching metal again. She dug her fingers into his neck, her grip strong and painful. It brought back unpleasant memories of Crew Cut's handling of him outside the music shop. If anything, her fingers felt even more like they were made out of steel.

Sensing his skyrocketing level of distress, Cindy laughed. "Relax. You're fine. Take a deep breath. It really would've been better if you'd just walked away from all this, but you didn't do that. You came here and you found me. Now I think I need to know what you know. Just so I can reassure myself. I think you're basically harmless, but I need to know that for a fact. Understand?"

Cole shuddered and managed a nod. "I think so."

Cindy smiled. "Good. Drink some of your beer and try to relax. Then start again from the beginning and tell me everything. Can you do that?"

Cole nodded again and heaved a big breath.

Then he started talking.

TWENTY

"THAT'S QUITE A STORY," CINDY told him after he fell silent, his tale concluded. "Most people would have trouble believing any of it."

Including, Cole thought, *the part that's happening right fucking now.*

It was another observation he chose to keep to himself.

"Do *you* believe me?"

She pursed her lips and made a noise of contemplation before saying, "I do. I'm positive everything you just told me happened exactly the way you say it did, but your perception of many of those things is way off."

"How so?"

Cindy didn't answer right away. She examined her fingernails, checking for chips in the black polish. This wasn't done in a cursory way. She did it meticulously, stretching out the fingers of both hands, then curling them as she looked closer. As she did this, Nikki's probing fingers crept closer to the hollow of his throat from both sides.

The pressure she was exerting was getting scary.

"Cindy?"

She didn't look away from her nails as she replied. "Yes, Cole?"

"Could you please tell your dominatrix bartender not to choke me to death?"

Cindy looked at him, her expression neutral.

Then she lifted her gaze, looking at Nikki for a moment before again making eye contact with Cole. "I'll leave that to her discretion." She glanced at the Heineken bottle grasped in his right hand. "You've barely touched that beer. Drink it. It'll help you relax."

Nikki chuckled.

Instead of lifting the bottle to his mouth, he eyed the second open bottle, which was still where Nikki had left it, near the front edge of the desk.

Cindy smiled. "They're both for you. I recommend having every drop. Enjoy them."

Another disquieting chuckle from Nikki.

"I don't think I will."

Cindy shrugged. "Whatever. I think it's rude, turning down a gift. But that's just me. I was raised well."

Cole opened his mouth to reply, but whatever he'd been about to say went unsaid, his brain beginning to short-circuit, overdriven by rising panic. Even now, with Nikki's fingers beginning to press into the hollow of his throat, a part of him wanted to believe he was misreading this entire situation. The beers weren't drugged. That was paranoia. The giantess behind him wasn't about to murder him right here in this office. She was only trying to intimidate him for reasons still unknown.

Except he didn't believe any of that.

What he *did* believe was that in that moment of eye contact between the women, Cindy had conveyed a silent authorization for Nikki to kill him in slow, torturous fashion.

Arriving at the edge of heart-pounding desperation, Cole at last managed to push out some words. "What did you mean about my perceptions being off?"

Cindy had returned to examining her nails.

Now she looked at him again. "What does it matter? You know what's happening here. Your part of this is almost over."

"I'd like to know what you meant by that. Don't I deserve some kind of closure? Don't I deserve to know the real truth about why I'm being fucking murdered?"

She sighed heavily, rolling her eyes. "Fine. I don't see what difference it makes at this point, but I guess I can give you that." Her eyes flicked upward a moment and the pressure on his throat eased off

ever so slightly. "Your understanding of things is all fucked up because most of it is shit you heard not even secondhand from a couple
of brain-damaged druggie losers. Did you really believe any of that
wild shit they told you?" She laughed. "I mean, come on. A heist at
the Vatican? A global network of spies hunting high and low for stolen artifacts? And that otherworldly shit? Jesus. I always thought you
were kind of dumb, but not flat-out fucking stupid."

Her every word radiated contempt, as did the sneer on her face.

"Well, I guess it does sound outlandish all said out loud like that."
Cole tried shifting in the chair, but Nikki still had a firm grip on him
and didn't allow it, her fingers digging in again when he attempted to
move. His voice hoarsened as he resumed speaking. "They made
what seemed like a really convincing case. And I did see the microfilm
reader. They weren't lying about that. It's in their apartment, so if
Tyler knew that and had something he wanted to—"

Cindy held out a palm. "Enough. Stop. Yes, Tyler did take a file
from Arthur Jamison's office. That part of it went down exactly like
you heard. It was a stupid fucking thing he did and it's caused a shit-
load of fucking trouble. Here's the truth. Arthur's an eccentric old
man prone to believing ridiculous things. He's a big believer in UFOs,
alien abduction, and ancient conspiracies. Bigfoot, for fuck's sake. I
have no doubt that file contained some weird shit a person like Tyler
could concoct a wild tale out of, one his dumbass druggie friends
would buy hook, line, and sinker. Also, yes, I guess he did use Zach's
microfilm reader, but I'm guessing those fucking potheads left out
the part where he made them leave the room while he checked out
the stuff he didn't want them to see."

Cole frowned. "Which was what, exactly?"

Cindy shook her head. "I know thinking things through to their
logical conclusion doesn't come easily to you, so I'll help you out. The
bumbling goons who missed not just one but two chances to take
you out today? They were after Tyler because that one remaining
piece of microfilm the moron kept showed Arthur Jamison, a man of
very advanced years, in compromising positions with multiple mi-
nors."

As soon as she said this, the many jumbled pieces of what'd felt
like the most confusing jigsaw puzzle all seemed to snap into place at
once.

He sighed. "Shit."

Cindy shrugged. "Yes. You see it now, don't you? How mundane perversity makes so much more sense than supposed proof of a ludicrous heist. Don't forget. I tried to spare you from feeling as stupid as you do right now. I'm not a total monster."

"I don't get why any of this means I have to die. I've never actually seen that piece of microfilm. I have no reason to go to the law with any of this. I'm not a threat to anyone. Jesus, it feels like your number one interest in all this is protecting Arthur Jamison. Why is that?"

Cindy took her feet off the corner of the desk and sat up straighter in the chair, giving the impression of someone preparing to leave. Someone who was done with him and ready to move on to some other piece of business. "If there are things you don't understand, so what? In life, you don't always get answers to everything."

She looked at the bartender as she rose from her chair. "Finish him."

Cole's eyes dropped, focusing on the still completely full beer bottle in his right hand. He had one shot at trying something and couldn't hesitate. The attempt was almost certainly doomed to fail. There seemed little chance his aim would be true.

But what the hell, he had nothing to lose by trying.

In as smooth a motion as he could manage, he whipped the bottle up and back, letting it fly from his fingers at what he hoped was the right point in the arc of his swinging arm. He experienced a moment of primal triumph as he heard a heavy thud followed by an ear-piercing shriek of pain. The bartender's strong hands came away from him as she staggered backward.

Flying on sheer adrenaline now, Cole surged up out of the chair and grabbed Cindy as she tried to go running by him. She shrieked and tried squirming out of his grasp, but he had too good a hold on her and threw her backward. The back of her head hit the back wall of the office and she dropped to the floor. A sound of rage from behind him made him reach for the bottle on the desk.

He was already swinging his arm as he spun back around. Chance smiled on him a second time as the bottle smashed across Nikki's jaw, exploding on contact as glass shards sliced open her face. She reeled backward and collapsed to the floor, spitting out chunks of glass and blood.

By then Cindy was on her feet again.

Cole grabbed the metal folding chair and swung it at her as she took another run at the door. The seat part of it smacked hard against her face and again she dropped to the floor.

Panting hard, Cole took a look around.

The women were groaning and writhing about on the floor. They were in pain and temporarily out of commission, but already Nikki was making another attempt to rise, if much more feebly than before.

Cole put the chair down and ran from the office.

TWENTY-ONE

A WAVE OF LIGHTHEADEDNESS OVERCAME him as he dashed through the open doorway. He staggered forward until he hit the opposite wall of the hallway. Bracing his palms against the wall, he tried taking a few sideways steps but that sense of lightheadedness became more pronounced and he began sliding to the floor.

Cole briefly retained enough awareness to understand that a period of unconsciousness—perhaps a permanent one—was encroaching. It was enough time to experience some moments of mind-bending terror. He'd summoned enough bravery to attempt an unlikely escape and for one exhilarating moment freedom and continued life seemed not only possible but probable. Then his body and mind betrayed him and once again doom seemed certain. Even as darkness descended, his mind worked hard to deduce what had happened.

That first beer.

Yes, that had to be it, the one he'd had out at the bar while trying to talk to the sullen giantess who would later wrap her strong hands around his neck. That beer must have been drugged, too, perhaps at a lower dose.

Cole sighed as his knees touched the floor.

He felt a tinge of melancholy pride on arriving at this likely answer.

Then the darkness took him.

~

He knew something was wrong as awareness returned, but at first he had trouble identifying the source of the wrongness while his eyes fluttered and he struggled to focus. Then the world snapped back into sharp relief and he saw the face of another person directly in front of him. The face of an attractive young woman with short brown hair. He had no idea who the woman was or why she was so up in his face like this. Then an intense sense of disorientation took hold of him as the secret behind the feeling of something amiss began to reveal itself.

He was looking at a mirror, a reflection, *not* at the face of a different person sitting directly opposite him. His breathing quickened and he leaned forward, staring harder at the reflected image. The woman in the mirror leaned forward at the same time, her eyes widening. Cole studied the mirror closely in hopes of glimpsing himself somewhere, but all the mirror showed him was the unknown woman mimicking his every movement.

He felt like he was losing his mind and maybe that was true, because from all indications his consciousness had taken up residence in the mind of this woman. Also, from what he could tell so far, *his* consciousness was the one in control. To prove this, he decided to perform a test. He raised a hand and gently touched his face. His pretty face.

For fuck's sake.

He waved the hand at the mirror, another movement initiated and executed by the consciousness of Cole Watson, who now existed inside this woman whose name he did not know. Warring instincts to laugh or cry flared up inside him. Both at the same time seemed the most appropriate response to this insane and impossible situation. He did his damnedest to hold back tears, however, because he worried an eruption of moisture might ruin the woman's impeccable makeup, and he wouldn't have clue fucking one how to go about fixing that.

An attempt to reach out to the woman's consciousness proved fruitless. He tried talking to her inwardly, but received only silence in response. Whether she'd been displaced entirely or shunted off to the side somehow was impossible to tell. He wondered if she might still be awake and aware in there, a prisoner no longer in control of her own body. God, he hoped not. He wanted to believe she was in a state of temporary mental hibernation instead, because the other option was almost too horrible to contemplate.

Whether this was really happening or a delusion occurring in the midst of a coma or blackout was impossible to determine. It *felt* real and so for now he could only go forward as if that were the case. He took a look around and determined that he was in a dressing room for performers. He was able to surmise this only because he'd seen such spaces depicted in movies and on TV many times. He'd never actually been inside one in real life. Until now. There was a rack of costumes and clothes and an abundance of makeup supplies on the surface in front of him.

Despite his overriding sense of alarm at this strange development, he found it funny that internally he was still thinking of himself in masculine terms, when, for the time being at least, he was something else, at least on a physiological level. He shied away from any attempt to parse the many and varied potential implications should this changed state persist, because he wasn't even close to ready to cope with that.

Then there was his new body's state of near total undress to consider. A flimsy piece of black fabric covered his vagina and perhaps a portion of his ass. He glanced down and saw a pair of sky-high black heels on his not very large feet. Pasties with tassels attached hid his nipples. Amidst the makeup supplies on the vanity station was a familiar black mask.

Oh, shit.

No, it can't be.

Before he could ponder yet another set of sanity-shredding implications, he sensed movement behind him. He turned his (her) head and somehow found the will not to scream when he saw Nikki come striding into the dressing room. He was sure he would again be forced to start fighting for his life, but now something else wasn't right.

Nikki was smiling and looked happy to see him. That was bewildering enough, but then the lack of facial lacerations registered. His state of confusion, already at a high level, now shot right off the scale. This time he reacted by doing the only thing that made any sense under the circumstances, which was to do nothing at all. He said nothing and didn't move a muscle. This stemmed from a deep fear of unintentionally giving himself away by speaking or acting in a way this woman, whose body he was inhabiting, would not.

The bartender walked right up to where he was sitting and gave his shoulder a gentle, affectionate squeeze. "Damn, babe. You're looking especially fabulous tonight."

Cole made a noncommittal noise of reluctant semi-affirmation.

She's not wrong, but damn, this is strange.

Nikki's hand was still on his shoulder, its presence there failing to calm his nerves even the slightest bit. All he could think of were those terrifying moments in Cindy's office prior to his failed escape attempt, this same hand closing around his throat with the intent of strangling him. He tried his best not to show how afraid the physical contact made him, but was not successful. The bartender felt his shoulder trembling beneath her gentle grip.

She stepped into the space between the chair and the vanity station, leaning against it as she put a finger to Cole's chin and made him look up at her. The look on her face showed only concern, with no deliberate attempt at intimidation. "Something wrong, Kate? You seem nervous."

So now he knew the name of this physical vessel. Or at least a version of it. He had no doubt Kate was short for something. Not that the precise moniker mattered much. At this point he was just glad to have a way of thinking of her other than simply as "the woman."

Staying quiet in the interest of not giving himself away could only work for so long. Now he needed to say something before the silence itself became incriminating. "I guess I'm a little nervous."

"Is it because Mr. Jamison is here?"

Cole didn't know how to reply to that. He assumed she was referring to Arthur Jamison, the mysterious rich man at the center of all the insane bullshit fucking up his life.

He was here.

But why?

He knew little about the man beyond the few things he'd been told tonight, but he couldn't imagine what about a club like the Hydra would appeal to an elderly eccentric. If it was illicit kicks he was after, wouldn't it be preferable to enjoy them within the private confines of his downtown penthouse residence?

Nikki was still awaiting a response, and a shift of her features communicated a rising level of impatience.

Cole again opted for a noncommittal reply.

"Um . . ."

Nikki sighed. "Yeah, I thought so. I know it's hard, babe, but you've got to play it cool around him. This is how you work off your debt, right? So suck it up and go do what you do every night. Get out there on that stage and shake that sweet little ass. Hardly anyone will be watching, anyway. Like usual."

Instinct told Cole that here was a point in the mostly one-sided conversation where he could actually say something. "Except for Mr. Jamison. Right?"

Nikki looked sympathetic, but spoke with firmness. "Of course, but you already knew that. Just don't think about it. If he does anything weird again, just roll with it as best you can."

By then, of course, another thing had become obvious to Cole. He'd seen Jamison already tonight. He was the old man in the suit who'd fired the revolver at the back of Kate's head and then later escorted him to Cindy's office. At the time, he'd believed the man was an employee of the club, maybe the manager, but now he knew better.

Arthur Jamison owned the Hydra.

Kate grimaced. "He knows how much I hate it. How humiliating it is for me. He likes seeing that, doesn't he?"

Nikki nodded. "He's a sadistic prick. You know this. Why is it getting to you tonight of all nights, after so many months of putting up with it? You're almost at the finish line, babe. One more week and you're done, your debt will be all paid up."

Kate frowned. "But what if he changes his mind? What's to stop him from going back on his word and deciding he's not done playing with me yet? I don't think I could stand that."

Cole realized he was experiencing an unusual level of agitation, a feeling he sensed did not entirely belong to him. He also belatedly realized that for a few moments he'd thought of himself as Katelyn instead of Cole. Was this a sign of the woman's own consciousness beginning to reassert control? If so—and if it progressed—what would happen to him once his own consciousness was inevitably given the boot? There were several possibilities he could think of right off the bat, almost all of them scary as hell.

All remaining warmth drained from Nikki's face.

"In that case, I'd get to enjoy your company here a while longer, which wouldn't be the worst thing in the world."

Katelyn sniffled. "You wouldn't stand up for me?"

Nikki laughed. "Of course not. I like you, Kate. You know that. But I don't like you enough to go against Arthur Jamison."

"What if he told you to hurt me?"

Nikki shrugged. "Then you'd get hurt."

More sniffling from Katelyn.

Someone stepped inside the dressing room and rapped knuckles against the open door. "Did I feel my ears burning? Were you ladies talking about little old me?"

Cole felt fuzzy-headed as he caused Katelyn's head to turn in the direction of this new voice. Standing just inside the doorway was Arthur Jamison. He licked his lips in a way that gave him an almost reptilian appearance, the tongue flicking out and retracting in the span of less than a second. The unabashed way his slimy gaze lingered on the naked flesh of the dancer induced a shiver of revulsion. Gripped loosely in his right hand and pointed at the floor was the same revolver Cole had seen him fire at Katelyn's head earlier.

Only . . . well . . . that wasn't really "earlier", was it?

Some things were becoming clearer despite the fuzziness that was continuing to overtake his consciousness. Nikki's missing facial lacerations had a relatively simple explanation. Everything else was a giant fucking mystery, but now that part made sense. The damage to her face wasn't there because the fight in the office hadn't happened yet. This entire backstage drama was unfolding *before* Cole's arrival at the Hydra.

So, in addition to moving from one physical vessel to another, his consciousness had traveled backward in time.

The concept made Cole's brain feel close to breaking.

Arthur Jamison came further into the room, raising the gun now and waving it around a bit with the barrel aimed at the ceiling. His face turned blurry and his voice sounded like it was coming from the far end of a long tunnel as he said, "I wanted to propose a bit of theater for your act tonight, dear. A little . . ."

The rest of whatever he was saying sounded like it was coming from under water.

Indecipherable.

Then Cole was back inside the darkness.

TWENTY-TWO

THE FIRST THING HE WAS aware of, as consciousness again returned, was a feeling of pressure. In another moment, it came to him that this physical sensation was the feeling of his cheek pressed against a flat surface. He opened his eyes and saw a wall painted a grime-smeared shade of beige. This space was a hallway and at the end of it was a square of blackness tinged with a faint glimmer of light. Loud guitar-based music was coming from that direction, a song he needed about one second to recognize as Sonic Youth's "Teen Age Riot."

Hearing a crashing sound from somewhere behind him, Cole pushed away from the wall and turned his head in the opposite direction. What he saw then sent a fresh surge of adrenaline spiking through his system. Nikki was face down on the floor, with only her torso visible through the open doorway. She'd stumbled while trying to give chase, probably still woozy from being hit in the face twice with beer bottles.

Blood leaked from the cuts to her face as she lifted her head off the floor and turned her glassy eyes in his direction. "I'm going to kill you."

There was a chilling amount of conviction in that voice. Hearing that tone of murderous rage left no doubt she was fully committed to following through on that threat. Her words were like razor blades slicing without mercy again and again into the most vulnerable parts of his already fragile psyche. They instantly wiped away any lingering vestiges of mental cloudiness following the restoration of his consciousness to his own body.

Despite his deep fear of her, some wild impulse caused him to look her in the eye and say, "Enjoy your new Franken-face, bitch."

Figuring he didn't have much time left before she regained a truly dangerous level of mobility, he then turned around and started running away from her as fast as he could. The first thing he saw as he emerged from the hallway was Arthur Jamison standing no more than a dozen feet away from him. The old man had his back to him and was facing the stage, watching as another scantily clad young dancer swayed about in a slow, languorous fashion suggestive of a drugged-out state. Her head was hanging heavily, looking as if it might roll off her shoulders at any moment.

Cole thought about barreling into the skeevy motherfucker on his way out of the place, but opted not to out of fear of the collision slowing him down. While he'd likely enjoy a moment of primal satisfaction by knocking Jamison off his feet, it was the kind of thing that could result in all kinds of thorny complications, including a fall of his own if the collision was jarring enough. He imagined a bunch of these art punk motherfuckers then coming out of their languid poses to pounce on him and hold him down until someone else could deal with him. Someone like Nikki. Right now all that mattered was survival. Playing avenging white knight could wait for another time, or possibly never.

Probably never.

He gave the old man and the tables in front of the stage a wide berth, ignoring the curious and mildly alarmed expressions of the judgmental assholes seated at the bar as he dashed by it. Then he was in the shorter outer hallway leading to the entrance. The bouncer with all the little bits of metal embedded in his face was on a stool near the door, reading an issue of *Film Threat* with John Waters and Kathleen Turner on the cover.

Looking up at the sound of Cole's approach, he dropped the magazine and rose up from the stool. The man held up a palm and moved to block his path. "Hold up there, little bro. I'm not supposed to let you leave."

Cole slowed to a trot and held out his hands in a gesture of apparent surrender. When he was close enough, he lowered his shoulder and threw his weight against the man, who lost his footing and toppled sideways, his head hitting the wall at an awkward angle. A sound like the snapping of a stalk of celery resulted. The man slumped all the way to the floor and made no attempt to get up.

Well, shit.

The guy looked dead. He hadn't set out to kill the man and, just like with George at the construction site, he didn't feel great about it, but he had to remember that these people weren't saints. He'd once again been put in an impossible position and he'd done the only thing he could.

Somewhere behind him someone called out his name. There was rage in that voice. Raw, murderous fury. It was Nikki, of course, up on her feet again and back on the hunt. Not quite right on his heels yet, but not far away either.

Cole hauled the door open and ran out of the club, making a beeline for his car. He'd just dragged his keys clear of his hip pocket when he heard Nikki scream his name again. She sounded like a wild beast and he was convinced she meant to kill him with her bare hands. It didn't matter that he was a guy and she was a member of the so-called fairer sex. He didn't stand a chance against her in any kind of physical confrontation. The terror gripping him made him glance backward and he whimpered when he saw how quickly she was closing the gap, taking gazelle-like strides with those maddeningly long legs. He might *just* make it to the Tercel ahead of her, but it was going to be a close call.

Which was why he changed course at the last possible moment and jabbed the key into the lock of the passenger side door instead of trying to get in behind the wheel. He just wasn't going to have time to get inside the car, get it started, and execute all the maneuvers necessary to turn around and drive away.

She laughed in a maniacal way. "I've got you, motherfucker."

Cole got the passenger side door open.

Crew Cut's gun was where he'd left it hours earlier, right there on the passenger seat. He grabbed it, turned around fast, and aimed it straight at the bleeding face of his wild-eyed pursuer.

Nikki stopped in her tracks. She was six feet away. One second longer to get this done and she would have been on top of him. A flicker of something that might have been fear passed over her face, there and gone so fast it might only have been his imagination.

She smiled. "You're not gonna shoot me, you pathetic little turd. Not out here in the open where people can see. You don't have the balls."

Cole tilted his head to see past her.

Perhaps a dozen patrons had filtered out of the club and were standing around by the entrance, waiting to see what might happen. Several were sipping their drinks. Most of those drinks weren't beers. They were fancy cocktails with olives and other garnishes. This was just another part of the evening's entertainment for them. The jaded fucks.

He locked eyes with Nikki again. "Any day before today you'd be right. No doubt about it. The thing is, today isn't any ordinary god-damn day. It's a fucked up beyond any hope of recognition kind of day. I've seen some shit, you psycho bitch, and I'm sorry, but I just don't have time for this."

He squeezed the trigger.

The gun boomed and the bullet found flesh, blood flying as Nikki staggered backward and wobbled on her feet for a moment before dropping to the ground. Someone in the crowd by the door screamed, possibly feeling a slight shade less disaffected now.

Cole slammed the passenger side door shut and hurried around to the other side. He dropped in behind the wheel, jammed Crew Cut's gun into the glovebox between the seats, and jabbed the key into the ignition, firing up the engine. Someone else started screaming as he worked the gear shifter, the sound closer than before, but he ignored it as he worked on getting the Tercel turned around and pointed away from the club.

The screaming was even closer, almost right up in his ear, it seemed.

Cole didn't care.

He hit the gas.

And then he gasped in surprise and hit the brake, because there she was, right in front of him, with her hands braced against the hood of his car.

Kate.

"Take me with you!" she screamed, eyes wide and begging. "Please!"

She was wearing a sleeveless black dress now with a plunging neckline. The strap of a small duffel bag was slung over one of her shoulders. Cole stared dumbly at her for a moment with his mouth open, until he realized he didn't have time to weigh all the pros and cons of granting her wish. He'd just shot a person in a parking lot in front of a bunch of witnesses.

It was past time to get gone.

He looked her in the eyes and nodded.

Katelyn scrambled away from the front of the car and got in on the passenger side.

Cole hit the gas again and this time his foot stayed down for a while.

TWENTY-THREE

COLE GAVE THE STEERING WHEEL a hard spin as the Tercel came rocketing out of the club's parking lot. There was no time to check for oncoming traffic and he missed colliding with an old Chevy Caprice by mere inches. The other car was passing by on Winston Avenue at a moderate speed and veered out of the way at the last possible moment. There was a loud thump as the Caprice bumped over the curb on the opposite side of the street, a sound followed by a pop signaling the bursting of a tire and then the loud blaring of a horn.

Cole never slowed down.

He kept spinning the wheel until the Tercel was pointed straight down the street, heading back in the direction from which he'd come no more than thirty minutes earlier, give or take. Leaving aside the weird variable of his time spent inside the body of the girl now riding shotgun, that is. He didn't slow down until he neared the end of the blighted street, and that was only long enough to gauge the relative safety of another high-speed spin into the cross street. This time there were no oncoming cars—at least none near enough to present an immediate threat of mortal danger—and so he again executed the same risky maneuver, cranking the wheel hard as he took a wide, looping turn all the way across two lanes before sliding back into the correct one.

Katelyn put a hand to her chest as she let out a big breath. "Oh, my God. You're a maniac."

Cole kept the gas pedal pinned to the floor as more decrepit old buildings and vacant lots flashed by to either side of them. "I'm just desperate."

"That makes two of us."

Two blocks blurred by. Then three and then four. At one point Cole blew through a four-way stop intersection without slowing down. Horns blared. His passenger whimpered and pressed her back against the seat. She glanced at the door mirror on her side and looked at him.

"Nobody's following us."

Cole nodded. "Okay. That's good."

"So you might want to slow down before you get us killed, or before some cop sees you tearing your way through town like Mario Andretti on crack."

Cole grunted. "Those are good points."

He pried his foot off the gas pedal and worked the brake until the Tercel was cruising along at a saner speed. A glance at the rearview mirror verified lack of obvious pursuit. He let out a shuddery breath and again applied pressure to the brake, slowing down even more.

They drove on in silence for an extended period as Cole took a random series of turns down various east side streets. A few street names he recognized, but several others he did not. He wasn't worried about getting lost. The way the streets were laid out in this part of the city made it easy to get back over to Gallatin, the main traffic artery on this side of the river. Getting out to the interstate from there would be easy, should he decide to hightail it out of the city, a move that might be the wisest course of action at this point.

Katelyn's presence complicated things, though.

He looked at her when they stopped at a red light. "Okay, I got you out of there. What now? There any place you want me to take you?"

Her brow knitted as she appeared to think about it.

Instead of answering right away, she unzipped the duffel bag that was now in her lap. She dug around inside it a moment before extracting a pack of Camels and a Zippo. "Mind if I smoke? I need to calm my nerves."

Cole shrugged. "Sure. Mind if I bum one?"

She shook out two filterless cigarettes and stuck both between her lips, lighting them at the same time. One stayed between her lips and the other she passed to Cole, who tasted her lipstick when he wedged it into a corner of his own mouth. He wasn't a big smoker, except when he was drunk in social settings, which was a lot.

Katelyn rolled down her window and exhaled smoke through the opening. "I guess just hanging at your place until I figure shit out isn't an option."

Cole took his foot off the brake and drove through the intersection as the light turned green. "I'd absolutely be cool with that if I was in a normal living situation, but that is not the case. I'm at my parents' house right now and I don't know how good an idea it'd be to show up there tonight with some chick they've never seen before."

She glanced at him, frowning. "How old are you?"

He groaned. "I'm twenty-six. For a little bit longer, anyway. Look, I know what you're thinking and you're not totally wrong. I'm too old to be living at home. It's complicated, okay? I lost my last job months ago and had to move out of my apartment. It's definitely not a permanent situation. I'll get my own place again whenever I finally get my shit together, but until then . . ."

She blew smoke out the window again. "Whatever. That's your business. I only meant you were too old to give a shit what your parents think about you bringing some girl home. *Any* girl."

The conversation was in danger of entering potentially uncomfortable territory. Katelyn seemed cool and, as always when talking to an opposite gender person he liked or found attractive, he was reluctant to cop to being a complete loser whose so-called "love life" was a desolate wasteland, a sad state of affairs that showed no signs of changing for the better any time soon.

She reached over and touched his wrist, which was resting near the gear shifter. "It's okay. You don't have to explain anything else. I can feel how uptight you are, so just relax." She took her hand away and flicked her half-smoked cigarette out the window. "I have a place here in town. I just don't think I should go back there. Like, *ever*."

Cole took one more drag on his own barely smoked cigarette and tugged open the ashtray beneath the radio, grinding it out in there. He took a right turn onto Gallatin and found himself pointed in the direction of downtown, which was only a few miles distant. He didn't know where he wanted to go just yet, but heading back that way didn't seem like a good idea, so instead he went up two more blocks and took another right turn down yet another side street.

"Do you have any kind of plan in mind, or are we just going to drive around aimlessly the rest of the night?"

Cole shrugged. "I have some friends who all share an apartment in Antioch. Three guys I grew up with in the old neighborhood." He laughed softly, without humor. "To which I have fucking returned. We could either just show up there or find a phone and see what they're up to tonight. If they're home, we could hang out there long enough to figure some shit out."

Katelyn smirked. "So your friends won't be upset if you show up with some strange girl?"

Cole laughed. "No."

They'll be shocked out of their goddamn minds, but they won't care.

Soon they turned down a street with well-lit gas stations on opposite corners from each other. Cole opted for the Exxon on the right-hand side of the street, pulling the Tercel up to a pay phone in a corner of the parking lot. He opened the middle glove box and pushed Crew Cut's gun out of the way to dig out some change. There were no quarters, but he managed to find two dimes and a nickel amidst the copper ocean of pennies.

Katelyn eyed the gun. "I can't believe you shot Nikki."

Cole grunted. "Believe it or not, it's not even that high on the list of fucked-up, unbelievable shit I've been through today."

She touched his wrist again. "Oh, I know. I know."

He glanced up from the glove box, meeting her gaze.

What he saw in her eyes confirmed what he'd already detected in her tone. "You do?"

She nodded. "I felt you enter my mind and take control of my body."

Cole closed the glove box. He stared at her without saying anything for a while, several minutes elapsing as other people went in and out of the gas station, a steady stream of cars moving through the parking lot. She didn't look away once the whole time, her eyes boring into him in an intense way. A part of him hoped she'd be the one to break the silence, but that didn't happen.

In the aftermath of their flight from the Hydra, there hadn't been much time to think about the strange occurrence that linked them. As the silence stretched out, he reviewed his memories of the event and became profoundly unsettled all over again. No matter how hard he tried, he couldn't come up with a way of explaining it that he could understand. Entering another person's mind shouldn't even be possible, yet it had happened.

He cleared his throat. "Huh. That's . . . interesting. As soon as I knew I was in someone else's body, I tried communicating with . . . well, with you. But I didn't sense you in there at all. Not until you started taking over again. Wait. How did you know that was me? Did you, like, look into my thoughts or something? Because no offense, that would kind of freak me the fuck out."

Katelyn shook her head. "No. I knew someone else was in my head and in control, but nothing else. Then, later, I saw you go running out of the club. I was in one of the booths. It was like a bolt of lightning hit me and suddenly I just *knew*. You were my mental intruder. It was a moment of intense soul connection. I'm surprised you didn't feel anything."

"I was kind of busy trying not to get killed."

She started shaking another cigarette out of her pack. "Anyway, I couldn't let you disappear without talking to you, so I ran out to the parking lot. And now here we are."

Cole laughed. "Yeah, here we are. On the run, like a couple of fucking outlaws. Are you sure you made the right call, chasing after me?"

She shrugged. "What's done is done."

Cole nodded. "You know, that might be the truest thing I've heard anyone say all damn day."

Katelyn lit her cigarette. "I'm a beacon of truth. I never lie."

Cole didn't know how to respond to that, other than to call her a purveyor of world-class bullshit, so he returned to the previous topic of discussion. "It's so weird saying any of this shit out loud at all, as if mental transference is something that could actually happen."

Katelyn sighed. "It *did* happen, though. Two people who never met before can't share a delusion."

Cole nodded. "Yeah. I know. It just doesn't seem possible, is what I'm saying. Maybe in movies or books, but not in the real world. Or so I would've said until tonight. So I guess my question is . . . *how* did it happen? Do you have any idea?"

She shrugged. "I do. Sort of. I'll tell you what I know, but maybe you should go on and call your friends first."

She had a point there. They'd been parked alongside the Bell South pay phone for a while now. Sooner or later someone else wanting to use it would pull up behind them.

Cole rolled his window down, leaned out to lift the pay phone's receiver off the hook, and fed his coins into the slot. After getting a dial tone, he punched in the number and put the receiver to his ear. The call was answered on the third ring and a slightly aggravating conversation ensued.

Then he put the receiver back on the hook and looked at Katelyn. "We're good to go." He frowned. "Fair warning. It sounds like some serious drinking is happening there. And I think they've got other people over. More than a few, from the sound of it. So if you were hoping for some privacy or peace and quiet, I'm afraid you're gonna be out of luck."

She turned her head and blew smoke away from him. "As long as we can get off the street and out of sight for a while, it's fine."

Cole nodded. "All right. Off we go, then."

He steered the Tercel out of the Exxon lot and started heading for the nearest interstate junction.

TWENTY-FOUR

THERE WAS NO MORE DISCUSSION about the incident at the Hydra until they were out on the interstate and several miles away from the heart of the city. A lot of the lull was rooted in Cole's need to focus on his driving. He'd consumed several beers by now and the last thing he wanted was to start swerving around on the interstate, highway patrol cops generally being quicker to pull drivers over than cops in the city. His main goal at this point was to arrive safely at the apartment in Antioch and hopefully stay the night there. Yeah, the open beer bottle between his legs maybe made him a bit of a hypocrite given what he was trying to accomplish, but whatever.

His headlights picked out a green highway sign informing them that the Antioch exit was five miles away.

He sipped some beer and cleared his throat. "So . . . you were saying you might know something about how that weird shit happened?"

Her face was turned away from him, her eyes on the dark landscape visible through the open window on her side, the wind whipping her hair about. A Heineken bottle was clasped loosely in her left hand. She looked at him and took a slug of beer. "Do you really want to get into that now? We're almost there, aren't we?"

Cole nodded. "I do, yeah. I'm worried we won't be able to talk freely about things once we're there."

"Why?"

He shrugged. "Privacy will be an issue. These guys are my friends, the ones who live there, but their guests might not be people I know. I don't know if I'd even feel comfortable discussing any of the messed-up fucking shit that's happened today with my friends, let alone strangers. They'll all be drunk as fuck."

Katelyn swigged beer again. "So? What's the rush? Maybe getting drunk as fuck is what you need most right now. I'll still be around tomorrow. We can talk about it then. Maybe in a calmer way than we could now. Wouldn't that be better?"

Cole sighed and looked out at the road ahead. He could see the exit coming up in the distance, less than a mile away now. "If that's what you want, I guess I can go along with it. To a point. You don't have to tell me everything yet, but give me something."

Katelyn stifled a yawn and sat up straighter in her seat. "I think what happened has something to do with the Time Keys."

Cole glanced at her.

Then he looked out at the approaching exit ramp and began the process of slowing the Tercel down. He refrained from an immediate response as he guided the car along the curving ramp. Once they were out on Bell Road and only a short, straight shot away from the apartment complex, he looked at her and said, "Time Keys?"

She nodded. "Yeah. Time Keys."

Cole leaned over the steering wheel and lifted his head to peer straight up through the slanted top of the windshield, his face twisted in a look of exaggerated concentration. Next he leaned his head out the open door window and craned it around as he again peered up at the sky.

Katelyn grabbed the steering wheel. "What the fuck are you doing?"

His head was still out the window. "I'm looking for the TARDIS."

"The what?"

Cole settled back in his seat and reclaimed control of the wheel. "The TARDIS. Time and relative dimensions in space. Because suddenly I'm feeling like I wandered into an episode of *Doctor Who* without even fucking noticing. *Time Keys?* Are you kidding me? That can't be a real thing. No way in hell. You just made that up."

She smirked, chuckling. "Actually, I didn't."

The entrance to the apartment complex was coming up fast.

Relaxing a little, Cole guzzled half his current beer's remaining contents. "Could you maybe explain what exactly a fucking Time Key is?"

"They're stolen artifacts. Ancient things."

So they were back to that again. The weirdness. All the crazy things Cindy had convinced him were just nonsense, the delusional fantasies of drug-damaged weirdos. Despite everything, there'd been an allure to the rationality behind her explanation. It'd been grounded in things he understood. Normal, real-life things that happened every day. Rich perverts getting caught up in sex scandals was something he could wrap his head around, as could anyone who'd ever perused an issue of the *National Enquirer* while standing in the checkout line at a grocery store.

Now he knew better. The weirdness was real and it was everywhere, lurking beneath the surface. Normality was the real illusion. He had only to look to his own experience tonight to know that for a fact. Forget the *Enquirer*. The world as he saw it now was more like something out of the *Weekly World News*.

Cole slowed the Tercel again and took a right turn into the entrance to the complex. He guided the car along a winding access road and then past the rental office and recreation center. A few moments later, after passing numerous residential buildings, he pulled into a space outside the one his friends lived in and cut the engine.

He let out a breath and looked at Katelyn. "You ready to walk into a den of debauchery?"

She zipped up her duffel bag. "It won't be the first time."

They rolled up their windows and got out.

After retrieving the remaining Heineken from the back, Cole glanced at Katelyn across the roof of the car and felt a moment of intense trepidation. Not because he didn't trust her. He did. As far as he could trust anyone he'd known less than an hour, anyway. What worried him was the prospect of what might happen once they were inside the apartment.

It was too late for second thoughts, though. Their course was set, come what may.

They started walking.

TWENTY-FIVE

AFTER GOING UP A FLIGHT of stairs, Cole led Katelyn to a unit at the back of the building, which overlooked the downslope of a hill leading to a wooded area. Music emanated from the apartment as they arrived at the door. Even heard from the other side of a door, the acoustic performance was instantly recognizable.

Katelyn sighed. "Nirvana. Of course."

Cole banged his fist against the door.

Seconds later, someone he didn't recognize opened it and peeked out at them, a sexy blonde chick wearing a flannel shirt and loose-fitting jeans with big holes at the knees. She looked like a model playing grunge dress-up, as if she heard the news about Cobain and instantly went through her wardrobe in search of something appropriate to wear for wherever the night took her. It was an ungenerous and possibly unfair assessment, but Cole had a hunch it wasn't far off the mark.

Cole said, "My friends live here. They're expecting us."

The blonde looked them over in an untrusting way, her gaze lingering longer on Katelyn and yelled into the apartment. "Spencer! There's a guy out here says he knows you. Some chick, too."

A voice yelled back in response.

111

Still looking less than happy about the intrusion, the blonde opened the door wider and said, "Whatever. Come in, I guess."

They went inside and Cole led the way down a short hallway into the living room, where several people were seated on the carpeted floor in front of the entertainment center, watching the 35-inch Sony television recently purchased by the roommates. The group on the floor consisted of his friends and some more people who, like the blonde at the door, he didn't recognize. These were mostly girls he figured Spencer knew from working as a bellboy at the Embassy Suites hotel downtown. Dustin and Tucker, his other friends here, did okay with the ladies, but Spencer was the real womanizer of the group. He drew the attention of girls wherever he went. It wasn't a hard thing to figure out, as he was good-looking enough to be in movies. People often said things like that about him, that is, but Spencer had no ambitions in that direction.

There was one dude he didn't know, a rail-thin guy in grungy attire. He had longish, greasy hair he'd last washed at least a week ago, but he had male model looks beneath the grungy veneer. Another poser. He didn't look like someone his friends would choose to hang out with given a choice, which meant he was friends with one or more of the girls.

Playing on the television was a VHS recording of Nirvana's *Unplugged* performance from MTV. The small stage the band was performing on was adorned with numerous lit candles, an ambience someone had attempted to recreate here in the apartment, with candles blazing on virtually every available surface, including all around the television and the top of the entertainment center. A faint scent of incense hung in the air as well. Cole's mind immediately flashed back to his time in the stoner-centric apartment of the music shop guys, and their one lonely candle they'd dug out from somewhere and burned in honor of Kurt.

One of the other girls on the floor, a striking brunette in a purple crop sweater and a tiny skirt made of some shiny material, had tears streaming down her face. She sniffled and shook her head as she stared at the television. "You can really hear the pain in his voice. It's just so fucking sad."

The blonde who answered the door made her way over to Spencer, attempting to snuggle up next to him on the floor, but he shrugged away from her and got to his feet as soon as he spotted Cole. He had a big, drunken grin on his face.

"Hey, man! Good to fuckin' see you, dude!" He gave Katelyn an openly appreciative once-over. "Who's your friend?"

Introductions were made.

Cole went into the kitchen and stowed his beer in the already crowded refrigerator, which required moving several things around and removing the bottles from the cartons. As he did this, he heard his friend laughing and amiably chattering away with Katelyn, whose responses were much more restrained.

Once he had the beer storage situation squared away, he popped open a fresh Heineken and rejoined them at the edge of the kitchen. "What the fuck is happening here tonight?" He gestured with his beer at the television. "You hate Nirvana."

Spencer put a finger to his lips. "Man, not so loud." He chuckled. "I'm a big fan. For tonight only, if you know what I mean."

He glanced over at the blonde in the flannel shirt, giving her a cheesy wink and a thumbs-up.

Katelyn rolled her eyes, smirking in an amused way.

Cole started to say something else, but Spencer clapped a hand on his shoulder and nudged him away from the kitchen, steering him toward a hallway leading to the bathroom and bedrooms.

"I'm stealing your man for a minute. Hope you don't mind."

Cole grimaced. "I'm not—"

Katelyn shrugged. "Fine by me. May I use your bathroom?"

"Of course, yeah, make yourself at home."

Cole was unable to communicate further with Katelyn at that point because his friend was urging him to move faster down the hallway. Soon they entered the bedroom at the end of the hallway, with Spencer closing and locking the door behind them.

Spencer laughed and said, "Dude, that bitch is fine as fuck. Please make me the happiest motherfucker alive and tell me you're hitting that shit."

The guy had his hand out for a high-five.

Cole reluctantly slapped his palm, if only because he didn't want Spencer giving him shit for leaving him hanging. His friend was at that level of drunkenness where even a minor thing like that was apt to kick off a loud, stream-of-consciousness rant about the crucial importance of upholding all the little rituals and niceties required by social interaction lest civilization begin to collapse, leading to an inevitable takeover by primates as in *Planet of the Apes*. The specificity of this mental example was a direct result of Spencer having already done multiple variations on the theme at previous drunken gatherings. While they were always intended as humorous, people who didn't know him often took these rants the wrong way, mistaking them for genuine expressions of crackpot rage.

Like always, however, Spencer's laughter was contagious, and for a few moments Cole laughed along with him. He started trying to force the smile away from his face as he thought about Katelyn out there in the bathroom, imagining how she'd react to this interaction if she could see or hear it. Maybe she'd take it as a harmless case of guys being guys, but somehow he didn't think so, not after what they'd been through together.

There was no romantic angle to their unusual and thus far short-lived relationship, nor would there be. He liked her a lot, but nothing other than situational temporary friendliness was in the cards. She'd go her own way when it was safe enough to do so, after which he'd likely never see her again.

He was okay with that, but the why of it wasn't something he wanted to get into just yet. Let Spencer think his loser friend had mysteriously gotten a little cooler for a while longer. For at least tonight. Where was the harm in that?

Cole took a swig of beer. "It's complicated."

This cleared up nothing, which made it the best available response. In an effort to deflect focus in another direction, he again attempted to address the situation in the living room. "And by the way, I still can't believe you're going to this much trouble to get laid. It's not like you."

"Did you not see how hot that chick is?"

Cole nodded and guzzled more beer. "I did. She's definitely on another level, even by your standards. The Nirvana thing is still fucking weird. All you do is rant about how grunge is killing real rock music."

"Fucking right it is and it's a goddamn travesty." Spencer's big grin slipped away, displaced by a sneer of genuine disgust. "Go turn on the radio. We're in a different goddamn world now. Everything's changed from the way it was just two years ago. It's like some kind of goddamn black magic spell. Everybody dresses like a fucking bum. Heroin chic, my ass. What's chic about looking like a loser who sleeps on the fucking street every night? Nobody's having fun anymore, except maybe the gangster rap guys. Van Halen put it best when they asked, 'Where have all the good times gone?'"

Cole laughed. "The Kinks posed the question first, if you want to get technical about it."

Spencer rolled his eyes. "Shit, man, whatever. The Kinks were first, but the version by Dave and the boys is a million times better." He started pacing about the room, the way he often did when he was winding himself up for a rant. At one point he stopped and pointed an index finger at the closed bedroom door. "All those bitches just love Mr. Kurt Blo-brain, especially now that he's gone and offed himself. Good job, Kurt. Way to make being a downer cool, you brainless fucking bastard. You think chicks of that caliber will ever show David Lee Roth the proper respect again? Dave left Van Halen ten years ago almost, but to them it might as well be something that happened in prehistory. It's fucked up. He should be revered forever like the legend he is, not treated like a joke."

Cole sighed. "To be fair, even Van Halen treats Dave like a joke now."

Spencer stopped pacing and stared at the Van Halen poster above his dresser, a reproduction of the photo from the back cover of *Women and Children First*. "That won't last forever."

"You really think so?"

Spencer looked at him. "I guarantee it. Someday they will all see the mistake they've made and come together again, and on that day all shall be right with the world again."

"If you say so."

"You sound skeptical. I blame your years of being corrupted by punk music. Fuck. You actually *like* Nirvana. I still can't believe that."

Cole shrugged.

There was a weariness in the gesture that came from enduring many rants with a similar theme. After venting, Spencer's obsessions always circled back around and got regurgitated again countless more times. Unsurprisingly, it was most prone to happening when he was drinking. Cole could recite many of his recycled rants from memory at this point.

Spencer smirked. "Oh, and by the way, nice job of distracting me from what's really important. Where did you meet that chick?"

"At the Hydra."

Spencer did a double-take. "You actually went in that place? Why?"

"I was looking for somebody." Cole knocked back some beer and shook the bottle. Only a couple ounces remaining. He'd need another one soon. "It's like I told you before, it's complicated. Some weird shit happened today. Some *fucked-up* shit, to be honest."

"And the person you were looking for had something to do with this fucked up shit?"

Cole nodded.

A silent moment went by.

Then Spencer cocked an eyebrow. "Okay, so what's the rest of the story? What kind of fucked up shit are we talking about, exactly?"

Cole poured the rest of the beer down his throat and shook his head. "I'm not even gonna try telling you about it until at least tomorrow. Or whenever we're both sober again. I need you to be able to look into my eyes and see I'm telling you nothing but the absolute fucking truth, no matter how crazy it all sounds."

Spencer's squinty expression made it clear he was concentrating fiercely in an effort to fully absorb and understand what he was being told despite his high level of inebriation. Some more silent moments passed as he nodded and thought about it. And then he said, "Okay. I'm dying to know what the fuck you're talking about, but I think you're probably right." His big movie star grin returned. "But I'm gonna write myself a note, man. I'm gonna remember this shit and we're gonna talk it out soon."

Cole was already moving away from him. "Fine. I'm in dire need of another beer."

He opened the door and walked out of the room.

TWENTY-SIX

COLE HEADED STRAIGHT FOR THE kitchen and grabbed another Heineken from the fridge. He then returned to the living room, where he did not join the others on the floor. They looked up at him as he hovered near the edge of the group. A couple of the girls smiled in a way that might or might not have been fake, it was hard to tell. He was sure they weren't overly thrilled by the intrusion, but were too polite to say so.

The one in the flannel shirt did not smile when she looked at him. She hadn't been friendly from the start, but Cole figured she was extra unhappy with him for diverting Spencer's attention away from her for what she probably saw as an unreasonable amount of time. Dustin and Tucker again greeted him from the floor, albeit in a distracted way, each of them loosely entangled with their chosen female companion of the evening.

There was no sign of Katelyn. He'd gotten a quick glance into the bathroom on his way back down the hallway. The door was open by then and there was no one inside. His chest tightened with an unexpected twinge of distress. He'd left his keys on the counter in the kitchen. Disappearing while he was distracted would've been the easiest thing in the world.

Then the girl in the purple crop sweater looked up at him and said, "Your girlfriend's out on the balcony."

The blonde in the flannel shirt laughed. "Girlfriend."

Her sarcastic tone was hard to miss, but Cole ignored her as his gaze went to the sliding glass door at the back of the room. The vertical blinds were closed and drawn shut nearly to the end of the rod, leaving only a small sliver of balcony visible from where he stood. No wonder he hadn't been able to see her.

From the kitchen came the unmistakable sound of a fresh can of beer being popped open. Also emanating from the kitchen was Spencer's voice. He was engaged in an exchange of drunken babble with someone else on the cordless phone. The blonde glared in that direction. If Spencer wasn't careful, he could wind up blowing it with her.

Cole went to the sliding glass door and pulled it open enough to step outside. Katelyn looked up at him from a cheap lawn chair at the other end of the balcony. She had several unopened bottles of Heineken on the little glass-top table next to her, along with a bottle opener. One open bottle was clutched in her right hand. Her duffel bag was on the balcony floor at her feet.

She smiled. "Figured you'd be joining me out here eventually. Thought you wouldn't mind reducing the need for trips back inside."

Cole nodded. "You're a smart one."

"I have my moments."

He pulled the door shut and joined her at the other end of the balcony, dropping into another of the cheap lawn chairs. "What made you come out here?"

She shrugged. "Don't think you want me to say."

The balcony overlooked the hill at the back of the building. Exterior lighting rendered the treeline near the bottom of the slope partly visible. The view was as nice as you were likely to get in this part of Antioch. One night after a period of heavy drinking, he descended the hill, passed through the stand of trees, and sat for a while on a big, slab-like rock overlooking a shallow creek. He polished off a bottle of Southern Comfort and listened to the crickets and the water trickling. Some while later he awoke to find himself stretched out on the big rock, squinting against the bright morning sunshine. He rolled over and saw a lizard staring at him from a few feet away. Still a little drunk, he asked the lizard if it was the reincarnation of Jim Morrison, and the lizard chose that moment to turn and scuttle away, which Cole decided was answer enough. No one had come looking for him.

He got up and trudged back up the hill to the apartment, where no one remarked on his prolonged absence, even though he'd been gone several hours.

He sipped some beer. "Maybe you should go on and say it anyway."

She shrugged. "Fine. I don't like your friends."

"You've barely met them."

"Doesn't matter. I can read people like a fortune teller reads a crystal ball." She shifted in her lawn chair, turning toward him slightly. "A few minutes is all I need to know what I think of anybody. And I think you deserve better friends than these fuckers."

Cole frowned. "I'm guessing you heard some of Spencer's loud-ass bullshit. He gets hyped-up and belligerent when he's drunk. I've learned to tune most of it out."

Katelyn shook her head. "That shit has nothing to do with what I'm saying. I'm sure he's the least shitty of the bunch. But not one of them takes you seriously. I can see it in their body language, in the looks they give each other. In a thousand little fucking things."

Cole took a longer drink from his bottle and didn't respond.

Katelyn said, "You said you guys grew up in the same neighborhood. Was it in the city?"

Cole shook his head. "We grew up in a smaller town in a neighboring county. The neighborhood was miles removed from anywhere fun."

"So these are friendships of convenience. You hung out together because you lived down the street from each other. In a place where there was nothing to do but drink and get in trouble. Right? Be honest. Other than growing up in the same place, the only thing you've got in common with these fuckers is alcoholism."

Cole frowned. "You're kind of bumming me out now. Also, are you some kind of psychic?"

She took a swig from her bottle. "It's a tale as old as time, that's all. Remember when I said you didn't really want me to say what I was thinking? Was I wrong?"

Cole stared at his feet and said nothing.

Katelyn was also silent for several moments. She finished off the last of her current beer and used the bottle opener to pry the cap off another one. She got up from the lawn chair and went to the balcony railing, leaning against it as she stared out at the dark landscape.

Cole finished his beer fast and opened another one. "I get that you mean well. Or at least I think you do. But you're not gonna diagnose and solve all my problems in one night."

She laughed. "Oh, I know. Analyzing you is just a way of avoiding talking about myself."

Cole again opted not to reply. There was a lot he wanted to ask her regarding the specifics of her situation and the secret things she knew about the Hydra and Arthur Jamison, but she'd been so adamant about saving that conversation for the next day, when he was sober.

She turned around and put her back against the railing. The look on her face was different now, her brow furrowing as she eyed him in a speculative way. "I just had a crazy thought."

Cole waited for her to elaborate, but she just stared at him.

He cleared his throat. "Um . . . okay. So what is it?"

She smiled again and gulped beer. "I was just thinking about how there's no reason in the entire fucking world why you and I couldn't go get on a bus right now. Tonight. Go somewhere far the fuck away and never come back again."

There was a nervous edge to Cole's laughter as he shook his head. "You're right. That's crazy."

She nodded. "It is. That's what's so great about it. It's wild and impulsive. It's the opposite of responsible. Your so-called friends would tell you not to do it. But I'm completely serious. Let's go. Let's do it. Let's be vagabonds. Embrace a state of permanent slack and drift forever."

Her enthusiasm elicited more nervous laughter from Cole. "I just . . ." He shrugged in a helpless way. "I can't."

She came away from the railing and dropped to her knees in front of him, looking up at him with eyes that were wide and beseeching. "You don't really mean that. You're just scared. Let's have an adventure that'll change our lives forever."

Cole took a long drink of Heineken. "But my life is here. My family. Friends. Everything I've ever known."

She nodded. "Exactly. And what has that ever gotten you? You're making excuses when the fact is there's nothing tying you here. No job. No place of your own. No responsibilities. No friends worth a shit. That's what you're not getting. You're as free as you'll ever be. This is the time to do something wild and crazy. While you're still young. While you still can. On top of all that, all the fucked-up shit you're dealing with now goes away by leaving."

Cole's frown intensified. He glanced out at the darkness beyond the railing. "Goddammit."

Katelyn smiled. "Yes! I knew I'd convince you."

He looked at her and said, "But why take a bus when I have a car? We should go in the morning when I'm sober enough to drive."

Her smile faded. "No. If we don't go now, we might never go at all. That's how these things work. You take time to think about it and your brain trips you up in a million different ways. Besides, your car links you back to here. Severing all connections is the only way this works. Believe me, I know a thing or two about disappearing without a trace. We can always get some cheap junker to ride around in wherever we wind up."

Cole leaned back in his chair and stared up at the balcony's slowly spinning ceiling fan. "I guess my big fear is you'll end up abandoning me after a few days. After the rush of running off is gone. And then I'll be alone in some strange place. I mean, I know you're not interested in me on, like, a physical level, so I see it as a real concern. Sooner or later, wherever we go, someone you *are* interested in that way will come along. And then I'll be in the way."

Katelyn's expression turned solemn. "No one knows what the future holds, Cole, but I swear on my daddy's grave, I will not abandon you, come hell or high fucking water. Also, don't be so hasty with your assumptions about me. I might just surprise the hell out of you. If that's not enough to set your mind at ease, remember this. No matter what happens, you will be okay. Even if things go bad, even if it all gets fucked up in ways I'm not seeing, you can always come home. Your parents would take you in again, I'm sure." She smiled. "Am I wrong?"

The way she said those last words told him she already knew the answer.

He sighed.

Then a tentative smile dimpled the corners of his mouth. "You really want to leave now? As in right fucking now?"

She nodded, grinning. "Fuck yeah, I do."

Cole laughed. "Either I'm losing my mind or I'm officially drunk now. Yeah. Okay. Fuck it. Let's do this."

And that was when the sliding door opened and Cindy Rollins stepped out onto the balcony.

She pointed a gun at them and sneered. "Hello again, fuckers."

TWENTY-SEVEN

THEY WERE HUSTLED BACK INTO the apartment under threat of being shot if they didn't comply. Once they were back inside, they were forced onto their knees in the living room with everyone else. His friends and their guests all had strips of duct tape across their mouths. They wept silently with their hands held in the air. The one exception was the skinny male grunge poser, who was sprawled unconscious on the floor, blood leaking from a gash at his temple.

Cole came close to fainting when he saw Nikki standing in the living room, the muzzle of her gun pointed at the back of Spencer's head. She was in a black tank top now that showed how muscular her arms were. It also revealed a Tweety Bird tattoo on her left bicep. A bandage on her shoulder told an unfortunate story—instead of landing the kill-shot he'd hoped for, he'd merely grazed her. Multiple lines of little white butterfly bandages stretched across the lacerated parts of her face. The look she gave him made him whimper, which made him sound weak and cowardly, but he couldn't help it. It was a look that said he was facing an endless amount of suffering, an ordeal that wouldn't end until he was begging her to kill him. Maybe not even then.

The recording of Nirvana's *Unplugged* show was still playing on the television, only now it was much earlier in the show from when he'd last glimpsed it. They'd rewound the tape and started again from the beginning. Cindy stepped in front of the television and aimed her gun at Cole's face.

"You're gonna come with us, you stupid fucking asshole, and you're not gonna try to run away once we're outside. If you do, I'm sending Nikki back up here to execute all these fucking idiots. Nod if you fucking understand."

There was a lot Cole didn't understand, but he nodded anyway.

Cindy smiled and walked up to him, whipping the butt of her gun across his forehead. He yelped in pain as blood spilled from a gash. "That's for not minding your own goddamn business." She whipped the gun around again, this time grazing his temple from the opposite direction. "That's for not accepting your fucking fate and causing all this trouble." She hit him a third time, smacking the butt of the gun against his nose, but not quite hard enough to break it. It hurt like a bitch anyway. "And that's for running off with Jamison property."

Cole wasn't sure what that last part meant.

Then Katelyn snorted and said, "I'm not anyone's property, you cunt. Not anymore."

Before Cindy could respond or attack her for the epithet, Cole heaved a breath and said, "How did you find us?"

Cindy smirked. "That was fate smiling on us in the form of your friend's drunken dumbassery." She directed a sneering glance at Spencer. "Seems you told him about visiting the Hydra tonight, and about how you ran into some trouble there. So the fucking moron decided to call the only person he knew with a connection to the club." She laughed and looked at Cole. "That someone being me. Someone he thought he could trust because I let him put his dick in me once upon a time."

Spencer moaned and tried saying something from behind the strip of duct tape covering his mouth, but it was indecipherable.

Nikki laughed in a demented way. "He was wrong."

Cindy laughed, too. "Yes, he was. All right, let's get up out of here. We're finishing this business elsewhere."

Pressing her gun against the side of Cole's head, she grabbed him by an arm and dragged him up from the floor. She then turned him around and put the gun against the small of his back, prodding him forward. Most of his friends and their guests wouldn't look at him as he reluctantly began stumbling in the direction of the foyer.

All except Spencer, whose bleary eyes tracked him across the room for a moment before sliding away in shame. Cole wanted to tell him it was all right, that he'd made an innocent mistake, but in the end he said nothing. They'd be hollow words anyway.

Cindy turned back and addressed the rest of them one last time before departing with her hostages. "What I told this asshole goes double for each and every one of you. Once that door closes, we'll be out of your lives forever. That's if you mind your own business and don't call the police. Listen close, because this is important. My father is Arthur Jamison, the richest man in the whole fucking city. Are you letting that sink in? Good, because if you don't do exactly as I say, you'll all disappear and never be seen again, except maybe on some future episode of *Unsolved Mysteries*. Have a nice fucking night."

And then they were gone.

TWENTY-EIGHT

THEY WERE TAKEN BACK TO the Hydra, where they were immediately separated. The club had closed early for the night. There were only a few cars in the parking lot and no patrons inside the club. Katelyn was escorted to some other room by Cindy and a burly security guy, while Nikki dragged Cole into Cindy's office and beat him to the point of insensibility. His face felt swollen and puffy by the time she finally stopped pounding it with her fists. Blood and tooth fragments spilled from his mouth as she carried him out to her car, a red Buick Lesabre, and dumped him in the trunk.

She drove away from the Hydra and out of the city. He could tell by the change in the traffic sounds and the speed of the vehicle. They were going fast, way over the speed limit from the feel of it. The old car's worn-out suspension made the ride a bumpy one even before they left the highway. He felt like he was being bounced around inside a giant tin can. She hadn't bothered binding his wrists before tossing him in the trunk, probably because she no longer took him seriously as a threat after pummeling him so viciously.

Woozy from the beating and the alcohol in his system, he barely had any strength remaining, but he groped around inside the trunk in search of one of those heavy old-fashioned jacks that typically came with cars of this vintage. Maybe he could come out swinging when she opened the trunk, give the tall bitch one last scare before she inevitably wrenched the jack from his grip and cracked it over his skull.

His search, however, failed to turn up a jack or anything else of use and before long he gave up. The ride got even bumpier shortly after they left the highway, the suspension sounding like the tired springs of an old whore's bed on a busy day. The roughness of the jostling soon convinced Cole the car's wheels were no longer touching pavement. He pictured a rutted dirt road somewhere out in the country. He strongly suspected he was moments away from taking a bullet to the back of the head prior to getting tossed into a ravine.

At last, the Lesabre began to slow down, only a little at first, but then down to a crawl. The car took one last turn, drove a short additional distance, and came to a stop. Seconds later, the loud rumbling of the engine sputtered and stopped. He heard a click and thought the trunk lid had moved. Then came a creaking of hinges as a door opened followed by a heavy thump as it slammed shut again.

Shortly thereafter, the trunk lid came open, and Cole stared up at his captor, who cut an impressive figure against the faint moonlight, her long black hair stirring in the gentle breeze. Despite her height and strength, she was all woman, her figure something a goddess would envy. Cole figured he'd have no problem at all worshiping her like one under other circumstances.

She reached in and grabbed him, cradling him in her arms as she carried him up to the porch of an old shack. The dilapidated structure looked like something out of a B horror movie, the kind of place where reading passages from the Necronomicon out loud would be inadvisable. She kicked the door open and turned sideways a moment as she carried him through the opening.

No lights were on inside the dwelling.

Her boots stomped across creaky wooden planks as she moved deeper into the cabin. Then she stopped and shifted her grip on him, allowing his legs to droop to the floor. The legs of a chair scraped across the uneven planks as she pulled it away from a table, the outline of which was nearly invisible. She dropped him in the chair and moved away from him, stomping off toward the back of the cabin. Soon he heard another door open, followed by some creaks that made him believe she'd descended some steps out back.

Cole looked at the open front door and tried to find the strength and will necessary to make a run for it. He had a feeling she'd left her keys in the ignition of the Lesabre, knowing there was no one around to steal the thing. They were in an isolated place, wherever it was. That was the thing about mid-sized cities in the south. No matter how congested and cosmopolitan parts of them seemed, more rural areas were never more than a relatively short drive away. If he could only get up and get moving, get behind the wheel of that fucking old car and start driving, he could effectively leave the crazy bitch stranded out here.

Long enough to get back to the Hydra and rescue Katelyn. He wasn't completely sure how he'd pull that off, no longer having access to the guns still stowed away in the Tercel, but he would try anyway, regardless of the consequences. It was crazy. No question. A couple hours ago, he'd never set eyes on her before and had no idea she even existed, but now she felt like maybe the most important person in his world.

Gritting his damaged teeth, he put everything he had into an attempt to stand the fuck up, but his ass still felt glued to the wooden seat of the chair. The sound of a generator kicking on came from somewhere outside. He groaned and kept trying to summon strength, but then he heard heavy footfalls as his nemesis came back inside the cabin.

Another moment later, lights came on as she flipped a switch. The old planks rattled and creaked as she approached him. He flinched when she put a hand on his shoulder from behind. She squeezed and laughed when she felt him tremble.

Then she moved into position in front of him and smiled. "Remember when you called me Franken-bitch?" She tapped an index finger against her chin and feigned a thoughtful look. "Or was that Franken-face?"

Cole spat out a glob of blood and it hit the dusty floor at her feet. "I think it might have been both. Or I called you a bitch after calling you a Franken-face. I can't remember. There was kind of a lot going on."

She punched him hard in the face, making more blood fly as his head snapped backward.

Then she laughed. "Yes. So much going on. It was crazy. Someone even shot me. Do you remember who that was?"

Cole shrugged. "Maybe it was the man on the grassy knoll, the one who really shot Kennedy. Or some rogue Vatican assassin looking for the Time Keys."

Nikki's nostrils flared, her hands clenched into fists. She was still wearing the fingerless leather gloves she'd donned right before beating the piss out of him at the Hydra. He guessed she wore them to protect her knuckles, which made him wonder how many times she'd done things like this. Until recently, he would've assumed she was too gorgeous to be a full-time enforcer. That, of course, was before her face got sliced to ribbons by the shards of a broken beer bottle, but maybe it was sexist to think that way. There was, after all, ample evidence of her capacity for brutality.

She popped him in the face again, making him whimper.

"Dumb boys like you are so cute when you think you're being clever." She smirked. "Or when you think you have some special, secret knowledge. You don't know shit about anything."

This was true.

Thanks to Spencer's possibly well-meaning but colossally stupid attempt to help, he never got to have that promised conversation with Katelyn, the one where she would reveal all she knew. Nikki didn't know that, though. For all she knew, Katelyn already told him everything. Nikki also didn't know about his brief time at the helm of Katelyn's body and mind.

He didn't actually need confirmation of all the details.

He knew the essence of truth. The truth behind the truth.

Something like that. Whatever.

He smiled, an expression he knew probably didn't look great on his beat-up face, but fuck it. "You're right. I don't know shit about most things. I can tell you a lot about underground music and movies, but what practical use is that to anyone? I get it. I'm a joke to most people. A pathetic Peter Pan. But I do know about the fucking Time Keys."

Nikki made a scoffing noise. "Okay. I'll bite. What do you think you know?"

"I know that until recently they were stored in a vault beneath the Vatican. For hundreds of years they were there, unknown to all but an elite few. I know Arthur Jamison stole them. Or hired people to steal them. I know they can be used to visit other worlds or planes of existence." His undoubtedly grotesque smile widened. "And I know they can be used to astral project and enter the bodies of other people."

The smugness drained out of Nikki's face as he said that last part. "What?"

It hurt to laugh, but he did anyway. "You heard me." This next part was in the realm of educated guessing, but he thought it was probably accurate based on his own experience. "I also know Arthur doesn't fully understand how to use the artifacts because things that ancient and possibly alien don't tend to come with instruction manuals. They're unstable, aren't they? Maybe prone to unleashing waves of strange energy? He should probably find a safer place to store them than underneath the Hydra."

She stared at him blankly for a few moments.

Then a small smile returned. "Hmm. Interesting. Maybe you know more than I thought. I guess Katelyn did some blabbing. She'll be punished for that, you know. Severely. It's too bad. I like her. But she only has herself to blame. You don't cross Arthur Jamison or spill his secrets. Everyone knows that. Anyway, I guess this is a good time to tell you what you already know. You're not leaving this place alive. I'll bury what you know with your fucking body."

Cole grunted. "Why didn't you just kill me at the Hydra? Why go to the trouble of bringing me out here?"

Nikki's smile widened. "Because this extra time we're spending together is a gift from Cindy. She told me to kill you, but that first I could spend some time paying you back for what you did to my face. As much time as I want, actually, as long as I get to a phone and check in once in a while. I have all kinds of fun tools and toys to try out on you, shit-face. This is gonna go on for days."

She punched him in the mouth yet again, hard enough to break off part of another tooth. In the wild unlikely event he got out of this latest mess, he was gonna have one hell of a dental bill. He spit out the fragment and it bounced off one of her combat boots. She wrapped her hands around his throat and squeezed until he thought he'd pass out.

Then she let go and laughed again as he gasped for air.

"I'm gonna enjoy removing you from the population, Quasi-modo. Your demise will probably raise the collective global IQ by about ten points."

Cole frowned. "I'm no mathematical genius or anything, but I don't think that checks out."

She sneered. "Nobody cares what you think."

She slapped him and turned away from him, heading toward a wall where various tools hung from pegs. Some were old and rusty, including a warped handsaw with a wooden handle. Other sharp-edged implements were new and shiny, some with price stickers still attached from the hardware store. There were traces of dried blood on some of them, confirmation that he wasn't the first person to be brought out here for a long torture session. This was the least reassuring aspect of the tableau, because it meant this was definitely a safe place to spend an extended period hurting a person while they screamed their lungs out.

Cole sniffled and started shaking again.

Nikki was halfway to the wall when the loud creaking of the floor planks gave way to an even louder splintering sound. The planks sagged precipitously beneath her. She had time enough to spin around and stare at him with wide, frightened eyes.

Then the planks gave way and she fell through a hole in the floor.

TWENTY-NINE

THE NEXT THING COLE HEARD was a heavy thump and a loud gasp from Nikki. Then came a moment of tense, eerie silence. After that was when the screaming started. Still sagging in the chair, he eyed the hole in the floor with a profound feeling of mistrust, unable to believe it was real, or that what he'd seen happen had really happened.

That shrill, desperate screaming sure sounded real, though, with the way it kept going on and on. As additional minutes elapsed, sobs and pleas for help punctuated the screaming. It was hard for him to believe it was Nikki down there making those noises, which could not be more different from the way she'd sounded prior to the rotting floor planks collapsing beneath her. He didn't know yet what had happened to her, but it had to be pretty bad to elicit such pitiful sounds from perhaps the scariest human being he'd ever encountered.

After several minutes of listening to her, Cole at last mustered the strength to slide out of the chair. He didn't like the sound the floor planks made when his knees hit them. The fear of encountering a fate similar to whatever had happened to Nikki felt very real. A vivid image of the whole place falling down around him and burying him in a pile of rubble formed in his head. It was possible he now harbored a misperception of the cabin's overall state of decay. Nikki might merely have had the misfortune of heavily trodding across a particularly rotten plank. Then, once that one gave out, the weight of her falling body caused her to crash through the adjacent planks as well. This theory made a lot of sense, but he wasn't quite ready to stake his life on it. If there was any chance the whole place really was on the verge of collapse, his best bet was to make his way to the door on his hands and knees.

With the intention of doing precisely that, he leaned forward and braced his hands on the floor. He took a big calming breath, slowly exhaled, and started moving toward the door. He'd only moved a few feet in that direction when Nikki started calling out to him by name, begging for help. She was crying constantly now and sounded like a frightened little child. He shouldn't feel empathy for her, not after taking so much brutal abuse, but it happened anyway.

The door was less than six feet away when he stopped moving. He stared at the opening and the sliver of dark woods visible beyond it. Also visible was the front end of the Buick Lesabre. He still thought it likely the keys were in the ignition. If he was right about that, all he had to do now was get behind the wheel and leave.

Deliverance from this nightmare was only a short distance away.

He sighed and began to pivot slowly away from the door, pausing twice before getting himself pointed in the direction of the hole. The pauses were to gauge whether the sharp creaks he heard were alarming enough to abandon this foolish notion that had seized him. Whatever had happened to her, there was little chance he could offer any real assistance, not in this battered condition. Regardless, he felt this was something he needed to verify on something other than a gut level. He needed to *see*.

After another calming breath, he started moving toward the jagged hole on his hands and knees, pausing several more times to test the planks for sturdiness. They groaned and creaked, but did not seem close to collapse. He kept moving. Nikki kept calling out to him. As he got closer to the hole, the creaking sounds increased in volume and he again debated abandoning this impulse to check on the wellbeing of the person who'd promised to kill him. Instead, he lowered himself all the way to the floor and began crawling forward on his belly like a worm. The creaking got louder still and one of the planks to his right, beneath where his palm pushed down, sagged in a way he didn't like.

But he was almost there. Two more feet.

He slithered forward and then at last arrived at the edge of the hole. Before getting a look at Nikki, one of the first things he became aware of was that his shoulders were now roughly aligned with a joist holding up what remained of this section of the floor. It looked at least somewhat sturdier than the floor planks, which was mildly reassuring. If nothing else, it'd be something to grab onto if this part of the floor also gave out.

After pulling himself forward a few more inches, until his head was hanging out over the hole's edge, he looked straight down into a dark, dank cellar, one that went down much deeper than he would've guessed, maybe as much as twenty feet. On the cellar floor was Nikki. She was on her back, staring up at him. The bottom part of her right leg was snapped in half, with the lower part jutting away at a sickening angle. A piece of her tibia was visible through a tear in her pants.

She sniffled. "Please help me, Cole. Please."

"Um . . ."

There wasn't a damn thing he could do for her, not without a lot of help. That much he knew right away. He also knew he had bigger things to worry about than summoning assistance for someone who'd never consider doing the same for him were their positions reversed.

"I'm gonna have to go. I'm sorry."

She whimpered. "You have to get me out of here. I'm hurting real bad. I can't fucking stand it. Please."

"I just don't see how that's possible. Even if I had a rope to throw down, I'm not strong enough to pull you up."

Not after having the shit beaten out of me, he added inwardly.

She surprised him with a single sob-choked laugh. "You don't even need to do it that way, silly. There's a pair of cellar doors out back. There's a chain on them, but no lock. You can pull me out of here. Drag me up the stairs. Please do it. I'll do anything you want. Just please do it."

The clear agony in her voice as she struggled to talk tugged at his heart, but it didn't change things much. "Come on. You're a big lady. Taller and heavier than me. I'm also in pretty rough shape thanks to you. Dragging you up some stairs isn't something I can do. I think you know that."

She got mad then, some of the former rage stealing back into her voice. "Then call a fucking ambulance! Go take my car and find a phone."

Cole sighed. "I don't even know where the fuck this place is. I was in your trunk on the way out here, remember?"

She did some more whimpering and said, "It hurts so much. So fucking much."

"I know. I'm sorry."

She cried out in pain as she raised up on her elbows in an effort to peer at him more intently. "You can do this. The road out here ends at this clearing. All you have to do is turn around and drive back down the road. Turn right on the first paved road you reach and there'll be a gas station a mile up ahead. You can call an ambulance from there."

Cole shook his head. "I need to go find Katelyn."

"Fuck that bitch!"

This enraged exclamation was followed by another loud screech of agony.

"I'm gonna have to go now. I'm sorry this happened to you."

She started sobbing again. "Please, no. I'm sorry for hurting you. I really am. There's so much I can do for you if you just help me. Money. Sex. Whatever you want. Come down here and I'll suck your cock right now. Forget Katelyn. She'd never fuck you anyway. You know that."

Cole recoiled from the image her words put in his head. It was hard to imagine the kind of person who'd take her up on an offer like that. Someone who'd just stand there and first take a bribe in the form of oral sex from a woman with a hideously broken leg before offering assistance. He was sure such monsters existed. The true crime magazines with lurid covers he always saw at grocery stores were proof enough of that. But he couldn't tolerate the idea of ever *being* a person like that.

"I'm sorry. I'm gonna go now."

She screamed. "NO! Please, no. Please. I'm so scared. So fucking scared. Please don't leave me. Please."

The rising intensity of her desperation was what finally prompted him to turn away from her and start making his way to the front door. She kept screaming and sobbing, calling his name. The floor creaked and occasionally cracked, but he kept moving, his course set now. He grabbed hold of the door frame and hauled himself to his feet, glancing back at the gaping hole in the floor one last time before turning away from it forever. He hurried across the porch and then down the steps to the ground, where he immediately began lurching his way over to the car. Nikki's screams continued to resound in the night as he settled in behind the Lesabre's steering wheel.

His gaze went to the ignition.

He'd been right about the keys.

The sound of the engine as he fired it up partly blocked out the sounds of Nikki's suffering, but he had a feeling a part of him would still be hearing those screams even after he was gone from here. As long as he lived, he might never stop hearing them.

Cole got the car turned around and started driving back down the dirt road.

THIRTY

IT WAS OTHERWISE A LONELY road with no buildings or helpful signs to tell him where he should go, but she was right about the gas station. The car didn't have a working clock and he realized he'd lost all sense of what time it was. Somewhere a little north of midnight was his hunch.

He pulled into the gas station and parked at one of only two gas pumps. It was just somewhere to park without pulling up right to the door. The Lesabre's tank was a shade over half full and he saw no reason to waste any of his money putting gas in a car he planned to ditch at the earliest opportunity. That he still had the cash he'd taken off the goons at the construction site had to count as something slightly more than a minor miracle, but he'd double-checked before turning onto the paved road and the wad was still there, along with his wallet.

Before getting out of the car, he checked his face in the rearview mirror and winced. He looked exactly like what he was—a man who'd taken one hell of a savage beating from someone intent on killing him. There was no use in attempting to clean up before entering the store. Even if he had wet wipes or a towel handy, it'd be a waste of time and effort. He needed to find his way back to the interstate and get back to the Hydra as fast as possible, before anything bad could happen to Katelyn.

Cole got out of the car and went into the store. He bought two quart bottles of Budweiser and asked the old man behind the counter for directions to the highway. The old guy took a long, silent look at him as he rang up the beers. He made change from a twenty and told Cole he looked like he'd gone ten rounds with Smokin' Joe Frazier. Some additional banter regarding his rough appearance ensued, but after some further prompting, the store clerk told him to head back the way he'd come. The road the store was on would take him right up to the interstate junction, which was about five miles away.

Back behind the wheel of the Lesabre, Cole buckled his seatbelt, opened one of the quart bottles, and took a long drink. He put the cap back on the bottle, put the car in gear, and drove away from the gas station. As he passed the turnoff point for the long dirt road up to the old cabin, he glanced that way and noted the signage posted— PRIVATE ROAD and TRESPASSERS WILL BE SHOT. He shuddered and hit the gas, zooming on by as he tried not to think about the woman still suffering somewhere up there.

Easier said than done.

Without medical help, he didn't know how long she could live with her leg all broken up like that. Probably not for long. One thing he did know, if somehow she did survive, he'd have to leave and go somewhere far away, live out the rest of his life under a new name, because she would definitely be out for revenge. He wondered if her gun was stashed somewhere in the Lesabre, maybe in the glove box. It seemed likely. Maybe he should head back up to the cabin and finish her off, remove the possibility of unimaginably horrific vengeance from his list of worries.

He laughed, shaking his head.

You just escaped from that hellhole and now you want to go back? Fuck that.

Once again, he tried pushing thoughts of Nikki out of his head. He took one more big slug of beer as he neared the interstate junction, put the cap on the bottle again, and pushed the gas pedal to the floor, grimacing at the way the car rattled as it picked up speed. Tightening his hands on the steering wheel, he kept the gas pedal down as the Lesabre hit the highway.

Twenty-some minutes later, he was back in the city. He needed another ten to get back to Winston Avenue on the east side. The flames were visible as soon as he turned down the street. His heart lurched at the sight of them, because even from blocks away, he knew it was the Hydra burning and not the porn store or gas station. Dread consumed him as he continued down the street, and he could feel the heat from the flames well ahead of his arrival. He started grinding his teeth hard as he tried his best not to picture Katelyn burned to a crisp.

He brought the car to a stop in the middle of the street and stared at the conflagration. This wasn't some small kitchen fire. The whole place was ablaze, with huge clouds of black smoke billowing up into the sky. There were no firefighters or emergency vehicles on the scene yet, but he imagined that would not be the case for much longer. The all-consuming nature of the inferno made him think it'd been set intentionally.

But who would do this? And why?

As if in answer to these questions, a shadowy figure came rushing out of a small thicket at the side of the Hydra's parking lot. The figure headed right for the Lesabre. Before Cole could react, the unlocked passenger side door was pulled open and someone dropped into the shotgun seat.

That person smacked a hand against the dashboard and said, "Drive, drive, drive!"

Cole's foot stayed on the brake pedal.

The intruder's head turned slowly toward him. "You're not Nikki."

Cole shook his head. "Nope."

"But this is her car."

"Yep."

The intruder frowned. "Where the fuck is Nikki?"

Cole shrugged. "She's bent out of shape about something. All broken up over it. Bottom line, she can't be here right now and sent me to pick you up instead."

Tyler Barnes sneered, confusion etched deep in his features. "Pick me up? I just saw Nikki's fucking Buick and figured I lucked into an easy way out of here. We didn't have a previous arrangement. Who the fuck are you?"

"You don't recognize me?"

Tyler snorted. "Your face looks like a pile of hammered meat, dude. No, I don't fucking recognize you." His gaze dropped to Cole's chest for a second. "Wait . . . I've seen that fucking Johnny Cash shirt somewhere."

There was a moment of silent eye contact as recognition dawned.

Then Tyler got back out of the car and started walking fast up the street in an apparent effort to get gone from both Cole and the disaster at the Hydra. Not knowing what else to do and in need of answers to many burning questions, Cole put his foot on the Lesabre's gas pedal and brought the car up to moderate speed. Tyler didn't think to glance back until the last possible moment and by then it was too late. The front end of the car gave him a hard bump and knocked him down.

After stomping on the brake again to avoid actually running over him, Cole reached over to the glove box and pulled it open. A thick driver's manual with a torn cover spilled out to the floor, probably because the compartment was overstuffed with a bunch of other ancient papers and assorted crap. And also, as he'd suspected, Nikki's gun.

He grabbed the weapon and sat up straight again, intent on retrieving Tyler and forcing him back into the car. Then he saw that the elusive son of a bitch was back on his feet already and loping away down the street, albeit with a noticeable limp now.

Cole groaned. "Goddammit."

He gunned the engine again and the Lesabre shot forward once more. This time Tyler glanced back in time to make an attempt to get out of the way, veering toward the sidewalk, but he wasn't quite fast enough. A corner of the car's front bumper clipped him, knocking him down again.

Cole reached for the gear shifter, intending to put the car in park.

Tyler popped back up again, like a goddamn jack-in-the-box. He wobbled away from the car, stumbling up the street, seemingly disoriented. Cole's hand came away from the shifter as he once again hit the gas, this time giving it a bit more juice. The car leapt forward and caught up with Tyler fast, hitting him hard enough to send him flying.

Cole stomped on the brake, put the car in park, grabbed the gun, and got out. He could hear sirens from somewhere nearby as he jogged ahead to stand over Tyler with the gun pointed at his face. "Stay the fuck down, asshole. Man, it's like you *want* to get run the fuck over."

Tyler whimpered. "I'm not an asshole. *You're* the asshole."

Cole snorted. "I beg to differ. *I'm* the one whose life got totally upended because of some stupid *fucking shit* pulled by you."

Tyler managed a whimpery laugh. "I don't even know what the fuck you're talking about. And *you're* the one who keeps hitting me with a *fucking automobile!* Asshole."

The sirens were getting louder. And closer. It wouldn't be much longer before the street was clogged with emergency vehicles.

Cole pressed the muzzle of the gun against Tyler's forehead and grabbed him by an arm. "On your feet, jackass. We're getting out of here."

"I'm not going anywhere."

In imitation of the way Cindy had pistol-whipped him back at Spencer's apartment, he smacked the butt of the gun against Tyler's forehead. In retrospect, he'd later realize Cindy was either simply smarter than he was or more experienced at beating people with guns. Maybe both. The safety was off and his finger was inside the trigger guard.

The gun discharged, startling them both.

Tyler screamed and rolled away from him.

Cole hurried after him and grabbed hold of the collar at the back of his shirt as he scrambled to his feet. The guy tried twisting away, but Cole maintained his grip on the shirt and swung him back toward the car. He jabbed the gun barrel against the small of Tyler's back and pushed him forward.

"No sudden moves, fuckwad. You don't want this thing accidentally going off again, do you?"

Cole let go of him long enough to reach inside the car and rip the keys from the ignition. Then they proceeded to the back of the car, where Cole got the trunk open and ordered Tyler inside.

Tyler glanced at the uncomfortable-looking space and scowled. "No fuckin' way."

Cole put the muzzle of the gun against his forehead again. "Plan B is I shoot you right here in the street and drive the fuck away." The first flashing lights appeared at the far end of the street. "You've got two seconds. One. Two."

"All right! Fuck you."

Grunting from pain and effort, Tyler crawled into the trunk.

Cole slammed the lid shut.

Then he got back in the car and drove away fast.

THIRTY-ONE

FOR THE SECOND TIME THAT night, Cole drove around aimlessly for a bit. He needed to take Tyler somewhere safe and private in order to conduct a thorough interrogation. There was so much he didn't understand and the asshole stashed in the trunk was his only hope of finding out anything, including whether Katelyn was still alive and where she might be now that the Hydra was gone.

The problem was he couldn't think of any good spots in the city conducive to what he had in mind. There was a remote chance he could break into an abandoned building, but it was too risky. He was not proficient in the art of breaking and entering, and if getting answers from Tyler required making him scream in pain, there was too good a chance someone in the vicinity would hear the commotion and call the cops.

There were lots of private places in the countryside, of course, including back in his hometown, the outer reaches of which were rural and quiet. He'd done a fair bit of driving in that area and could easily think of several good places to pull over and drag Tyler out into the woods for a no-holds-barred chat about things. The problem was getting there would require a thirty-minute highway drive, and that was just too much time out on the interstate with a hostage in his trunk. It'd be like begging to be arrested. Time was a factor in another way, too. His gut told him Katelyn, if alive, was still somewhere in the city. Tyler might give up the information he sought right away, or he might say nothing at all no matter how rough things got. Either way, the whole expedition would require an hour and a half at a bare minimum, probably longer.

Becoming frustrated, he gulped beer from the quart bottle as he drove and soon enough it was empty. He tossed the empty in the back and snatched the second bottle from the floor, keeping one hand on the wheel as he removed the cap. Despite the adrenaline rush from surviving multiple close calls, his beer intake over the course of the evening had reached a significant level. Keeping the car between the yellow lines was requiring an increasingly greater level of concentration. Still navigating his way through the maze of streets on the east side, he barely noticed the first time he swerved partway into an opposite lane and stayed there for several seconds. Until, that is, horns blared, alerting him to the danger. He jerked at the steering wheel, bringing the Lesabre back into the proper lane. Then, just a couple minutes later, it happened again.

"Fuck!"

A closed drugstore coming up on his right caught his attention and he jerked at the wheel again, tires squealing as he pulled into the parking lot. He drove around to the back of the building and stopped, taking a look around. There were no bums lurking around. None he could see, anyway. That was a plus. On the other side of an alley behind the drugstore was a residential house surrounded by a tall privacy fence. There were no lights on in the house, which was the only structure directly adjacent to the rear of the drugstore.

It wasn't ideal, being in the city and kind of out in the open, but it would have to do. He got out of the car and opened the trunk, keeping the gun pressed to Tyler's head as he dragged the whimpering asshole over behind a dumpster. This effectively blocked him from view of anyone passing by in either the alley or the one visible side street. God help him, though, if a cop out on patrol randomly decided to pull into the lot. All he could do was try to be fast about this and hope it worked out.

Cole said, "We're gonna have a chat right here. A quiet one. No talking loud or screaming. Same warning I gave you at the Hydra. Fuck with me, and I'll put a bullet in your head and drive the fuck away. But if you tell me what I need to know, you get to live."

Tyler was on his knees now, looking up at him through tears. "I'll tell you anything I fucking can. Just please don't kill me."

Cole pressed the muzzle of the gun against the bridge of his nose. "Where is Katelyn?"

Tyler frowned. "Who?"

The guy's look of confusion seemed genuine, unless he possessed stellar acting talent, which was possible. Still, Cole didn't think it was a look that could be convincingly faked under extreme duress. Maybe he was wrong, but instinct told him otherwise.

Cole sighed. "Katelyn. You must have seen her before. The beautiful dancer at the Hydra. Short, dark hair. Pale skin. Where the fuck is she?"

Tyler laughed. "You just described every girl who dances at the Hydra. Cindy is really fucking specific in her hiring practices."

"So they all have short hair?"

Tyler frowned. "Well . . . no." His frown deepened as he thought about it. "I guess there's, like, two girls you could be talking about, but I don't know their names. Look at me, dude. I'm not lying here."

Cole believed him. "How can you not know their names? Cindy's your girlfriend, right? You must spend plenty of time at the Hydra."

Tyler laughed softly, with detectable bitterness. "She never let me talk to the dancers. They were strictly off-limits. I wasn't even allowed to hang out there over the last week because of stuff having to do with her father. Until tonight, when she sent me there and told me to hide out in the dungeon. That's what they call the basement, by the way. And anyway, me and that bitch are officially no longer an item, dude."

"And why is that?"

More bitter laughter. "Because I overheard her talking to her father about me. I'd come up out of the dungeon because I was fucking bored as shit. About had a heart attack when I saw him there. Thank shit he didn't see me. Anyway, I heard her tell him she'd kill me herself. Like, basically in those exact words. No way in hell to misunderstand."

Cole grunted. "Why would she want you dead?"

"Because I'd become too much of a liability. Her old man gives her a lot of leeway in a lot of things. Indulges her. Lets her run the Hydra as basically a paid hobby. But he was upset with her, like truly pissed the fuck off, and that's the one thing she never wants."

Cole said, "Because you stole from her father. Don't bother

denying it. I already heard the whole story."

Tyler shrugged. "Yeah. I did it. Whatever. I was drunk as fuck at a stuffy old people's party and did a dumb thing. Cindy spent over a week trying to finagle a way out of it for me, but as of tonight, I guess she gave up and decided she was done with me. Easiest way to win back her creepy dad's approval, I guess. Anyway, I ran off."

"When was this?"

"Hours ago."

Cole frowned. "Did you start the fire?"

"Fuck yeah, I did." Tyler laughed. "You gotta understand, I was freaking out. I was marked for death. Maybe it was crazy, but I figured my best way of fighting that was noise and chaos. Get them all running around like chickens with their heads cut off, scared and confused as fuck. I went up to that gas station and came back with some gas cans and splashed gasoline all around the outside of the building. Then I lit the joint up."

"And you hung around and watched."

"Didn't have much choice. They did something to my car when I was in the dungeon. It wouldn't start."

Cole gnawed on his bottom lip a moment, a fresh stirring of anger rising inside him. "And people were still in the building when you did this?"

Tyler shrugged. "Don't give me that look, man. I'm no saint, but I'm not a monster either. The paying customers were all gone. I'd never have done it if that wasn't the case. Yeah, there were a few people still inside, including Cindy and her dad, but in case you forgot, they wanted to *fucking kill me*."

Cole nodded. "Right. And if a few other people got burned alive in the process, oh well, shit happens."

"I'm liking that look on your face less and less, dude. I see you've got your finger on the trigger there. It'd be way uncool if you accidentally fired the thing again, because I'd be dead for sure this time."

Cole thought, *And maybe you'd deserve it.*

What he said was, "Did you see if anyone got out?"

"Everybody in the building did, I think. Definitely Cindy and her fucking dad."

"And you know that for sure? You saw it happen?"

Tyler nodded. "Yeah, man. Like, seven or eight people came running out the front. Cindy and a couple of the girls piled into the old man's Jag with him and took the fuck off. One of the other chicks might have been the one you're looking for, come to think of it. The rest scattered."

"One of the other girls who got in the Jag had short hair?"

Tyler thought about it a moment before slowly nodding his head. "I think so. Maybe. But you gotta realize, I only got a quick look. Like, maybe half a second before I dropped flat to the ground. I didn't want them spotting me."

"Any idea where they might have gone?"

Tyler again thought about it a moment before replying. "My best guess is Jamison's downtown penthouse. I could be wrong, but it makes the most sense. The penthouse is his fortress against the world. I think it's where he'd want to go in the middle of a crisis."

"Could we get into it?"

Tyler laughed. "Um, no, dude. Don't be fooled by how easily I made off with that file. Getting into the building is a lot harder than getting out of it. Multiple layers of security, including codes you gotta know. And, no, I don't know the fucking codes."

Cole muttered a curse as he stepped back, taking the gun away from Tyler's head while still keeping it pointed in his general direction. All he kept running into in his quest to find Katelyn was roadblocks and dead ends. It was starting to get to him and his level of intoxication wasn't helping matters any.

Then something occurred to him. "What about the phone number there? Do you know it?"

Tyler sighed. "No, and it's unlisted, obviously. But I could get it. I'd have to call my dad."

Cole gestured with the gun. "All right, get up."

Tyler groaned as he got to his feet. He started moving toward the Lesabre when Cole gestured again with the gun. Cole said, "Where are we going?"

"We're gonna find a phone and make some fucking calls. What else?"

THIRTY-TWO

A PLAN QUICKLY FORMULATED IN Cole's head as he allowed Tyler to drive them to a nearby gas station. It was a plan with a foundation rooted deeply in deceit. He kept the gun on Tyler for this first stage of it as an obvious precaution even his prisoner could understand. Tyler became relaxed and cooperative because he believed Cole would let him go as soon as he had the information he wanted. He was so convinced of this he made no attempt to run or yell for help while they were parked in the back corner of the gas station parking lot.

Tyler got out of the car to talk to his dad on the pay phone. The windows were rolled down, but Cole only caught bits and pieces of the conversation, enough to know it was an agitated one.

Tyler dropped back in behind the wheel maybe three minutes later. "First time I talked to the old man in over a week. He was pretty pissed, but I got the number."

He recited it and Cole did his best to commit it to memory.

They sat there in silence for a moment.

Then Tyler cleared his throat and said, "So, uh . . . you gonna call the motherfucker?"

Cole nodded. "Yeah, but not from here. Let's go."

Tyler put the Lesabre in gear and drove away from the gas station. "Where to?"

Cole told him.

Tyler frowned. "Why are we going back there?"

Cole turned in his seat and pressed the barrel of the gun into Tyler's abdomen. "Just do it."

Tyler snorted. "You wouldn't shoot me while I'm driving."

"Did you forget I'm the same guy who ran you down in the street three fucking times? I'll do whatever I have to do. So just do it."

A worried look came over Tyler's face, but he did as he was told as Cole pressed the gun barrel harder into his flesh. A short while later, they were parked out back behind the same drugstore again. They got out of the car and Tyler made an immediate attempt to run, but in his haste he stumbled and pitched forward on the asphalt. Cole fell upon him before he could get up and start running again. Having learned his lesson from his previous experience in this area, he kept his finger outside the trigger guard as he whipped the gun across the crown of Tyler's skull several times, effectively subduing him.

At that point, he hauled the bleeding, beaten man to his feet and forced him back into the trunk.

Tyler looked up at him through teary eyes and pleaded with him one last time. "Please don't kill me."

Cole grunted. "I'm not gonna kill you. But you should know something. You did a stupid thing and a lot of people died or got hurt today because of it. You said it yourself. You're no saint."

He closed the trunk and got back in behind the wheel.

This time as he drove he resisted the temptation to resume drinking. There'd be time for that after this was all over.

If he was still alive by then.

THIRTY-THREE

HE PLACED THE CALL TO the penthouse from a downtown pay phone, one that was just a few blocks down the street from the place where he hoped Katelyn was holed up with the others. His heart felt like it was going a million miles an hour as he dropped his coins in the slot and punched in the number. He was hanging all his hopes on this one last move. If it didn't pan out, he didn't know what he'd do. He squeezed the phone tight, praying the call wouldn't go unanswered.

The call connected after two rings.

A voice from the other end said, "Hello?"

Cindy.

He felt relieved and intimidated at the same time, his heart still going fast as he said, "It's me. Cole."

A long pause. "How did you get this number?"

Cole said, "Does it matter? Listen, I've got a proposal for you. For you *and* your father, I guess."

Another pause.

Cindy moved her mouth away from the phone and muttered something to someone else. Then she sighed and said, "All right. Let's hear it."

"It's really very simple," he told her, keeping his mouth covered and head turned away from people passing by on the busy sidewalk. It was early morning hours now, but this was a popular tourist area and the bars were always open late. A lot of rowdy, loud people were out and about. Nirvana's biggest hit was blasting through the open doors of the bar directly across the street. "I know I'm in over my head and I just want out from under all this shit. I'm not out for any kind of revenge or win here, and I sure as hell have no interest in blackmailing your father, but I do have something you want and I'm willing to let you have it on one condition."

Cindy grunted. "Fine. Let's hear it."

He told her what he had in mind.

She put the phone down after telling him to hang on for a few minutes. While he waited, a recorded operator's voice told him to feed the phone some more coins if he wanted to stay connected. All he had left in coinage was three dimes. He dropped them in the slot, hoping they'd be enough. At last, Cindy came back and told him Arthur Jamison had agreed to his proposal. Katelyn would be on the sidewalk outside the high-rise that housed the old man's luxury penthouse. They could talk for however long Katelyn wanted to talk to him.

Cole told her where Arthur's people could find the Lesabre.

Then Cindy said, "You're describing Nikki's car. She wouldn't just let you go. Is she dead?"

Cole hesitated a moment before saying, "I didn't kill her. She had an accident at the cabin. A bad one. She might still be alive, but she'll be in rough shape."

Cindy made a thoughtful sound. "Okay. I'll send someone out to check on her. Just know that if she doesn't die, I can't control whatever she does or doesn't do. That's not a part of this."

Cole grimaced.

He didn't like that, but there was nothing he could do about it. "Okay. Listen, I don't know if we'll ever talk again, so be straight with me for once. All that crazy shit the record store guys told me was true, wasn't it? The Vatican heist and the alien artifacts, it was all real, wasn't it? It's the only way some of what I've been through makes any sense. Please, I need to know, if only for the sake of my own sanity."

This time the pause from the other end was so long he thought she might not reply at all.

Then she said, "You don't get to know everything. That's just how real life goes sometimes."

The note of finality in her voice made it clear pressing her on the subject would be pointless.

She said, "Are we done?"

Cole frowned. "One more thing. Why don't you use your father's name?"

The line went dead.

One more mystery he'd probably never solve.

Whatever.

He put the phone on the hook and started walking up the street. A part of him worried he was walking into a trap. He was on Arthur's territory now, after all. Even with witnesses around, his men would have little trouble apprehending him if they decided to go that way. Cole decided it didn't matter. He'd spent his life afraid of taking chances. Not this time.

Katelyn was already on the sidewalk outside the high-rise by the time he arrived. To his relief, there were no obvious hired goons lurking in the vicinity. She was still wearing the same little black dress, but now dark sunglasses hid her eyes. This being the dead of night, that struck him as slightly strange, until he realized it was probably to hide evidence of a beating.

She walked right up to him and threw her arms around him, laughing when he stiffened in her embrace. "I'm so happy to see you, Cole. I was so worried." She broke the clinch and laughed as she moved back a step. "Sorry. I know physical contact makes you uncomfortable."

Cole's face reddened. "Um . . ."

She smiled. "Which is totally fine. I really am happy to see you and know you're safe. It's not what I expected."

Cole nodded. "It was touch and go there for a while, but I'm okay."

An awkward silence fell between them for a few moments. While it was happening, Cole felt almost too acutely aware of how little they knew about each other. He couldn't begin to guess what was going through her mind, which was unsettling after going to such desperate lengths to find her.

Katelyn pursed her lips and tilted her head, studying him closely from behind the dark shades. "So . . . is that it? You don't have anything else to say to me?"

Cole's heart started racing again. He was afraid to say the thing he wanted to say and almost had to force the words out. "I was thinking about what you said before. About taking off and having an adventure somewhere far away. Do you still want to do that? Because I do."

She stared at him without speaking for what felt like an eternity. He was convinced he was facing rejection until she said, "Yes, I want to run away with you, but I can't do it tonight." She stepped closer again, until they were separated by only a few inches, but still without touching. "I still owe Arthur a debt. He holds something pretty serious over my head, the safety of people I care deeply about. I've agreed to do this one last thing. Make one last little fetish movie for him. We're gonna film it when I go back up. And then I'll be free."

Cole frowned. "Fetish movie?"

She smiled and touched his cheek, letting the touch linger this time, the gentle glide of her fingertips soothing to his swollen flesh. "Don't worry your pretty little head over that. Stay focused on what's important. I'm going back up now, but I want you to meet me at the downtown Greyhound station tomorrow. Noon on the dot. You got that?"

Cole was still frowning, but he nodded. "Yeah. I got it."

She kissed him lightly on the mouth and said, "Then that's when we'll see each other again. Don't be late."

She turned away from him then and started walking at a brisk pace back toward the high-rise. In another moment, she disappeared through the entrance and was gone.

THIRTY-FOUR

COLE STARTED WALKING BACK DOWN the street. His plan was to get to Broadway and hail a cab. There were always several lingering in that area, waiting to scoop up drunken tourists spilling out of the bars and whisk them back to their hotels. Finding a driver willing to take him out to Antioch would be the hard part, but throwing some extra cash around should take care of that.

He was halfway to Broadway when he noticed the white Winnebago coming up the street. It was one of the big old ones, with a large powder-blue W painted on the side. He paid it little mind until it stopped right next to him and a man with a shotgun popped out the side door and pointed the weapon at him. The guy was wearing a large and fuzzy rabbit head mask that covered his entire head. Though he couldn't see the face behind the mask, the skinny shotgun wielder's identity was given away by his Sub Pop t-shirt.

Cole sighed. "I do not need this shit right now, Jeremy. I'm sorry about knocking over the beer cans."

Jeremy jabbed the shotgun at him in a more emphatic way. "This isn't about the beer-a-mid, motherfucker! Get in the RV!"

Cole glanced at the Winnebago's open side door. "You know, I don't think I'm gonna do that."

The flow of pedestrian tourist traffic continued unabated around them on the sidewalk, with most people seemingly unperturbed by the strange drama playing out in their vicinity. Some probably assumed it was either a promotional stunt or weird performance art of some kind. Such things were not unheard of in this part of town, even at so late an hour. Cole figured the ridiculous fuzzy rabbit head mask contributed to this impression. The people passing by so nonchalantly might take a different view of things if they knew the unhinged dude waving a shotgun around in the middle of a tourist district was tripping on acid. Then again, maybe not.

Cole's failure to comply was making Jeremy more distraught by the moment. He started making hooting noises and jumping up and down like a pogo dancer at a punk show. What made this extra weird was the stark contrast between the wild way the guy was behaving and his far more laid-back demeanor from earlier in the day. Even after shooting the thugs at the Sound Stack, he'd been nowhere near this demonstrative.

A few people were stopping now to take in the increasingly absurd display. Some even had Instamatic cameras out and were starting to frame up pictures. Cole put a hand to the side of his face and put his back to the people with cameras.

"All right, man, fuck it. Let's do this."

Cole hurried through the RV's open side door and took a seat on a couch in the living area that comprised the vehicle's middle section. Jeremy backed into the RV while still waving the shotgun at the people on the sidewalk. He pulled the door shut and looked to the front of the vehicle, where a larger person wearing a rubber Ronald Reagan mask was ensconced behind the steering wheel.

"What's up, Zach?"

The Ronald Reagan mask turned briefly toward Cole. "Hello, slayer of beer-a-mids. How fortuitous to encounter you traveling alone along this dark and dangerous road so verily plagued by bandits and trolls. Art thou ready to repent for thy wicked deeds and walk the righteous path of ass-kicking truth-seekers?"

"Why are you talking like that?"

"Like what?"

Cole said, "Like you're on your way to a fucking Ren Faire."

One of Jeremy's hands came away from the shotgun as he swung the weapon about, thrusting the double barrels at the windshield. "We're not on our way to a fucking Ren Faire! We've come to storm the castle of the evil king!"

Cole nodded. "Riiiiight. And what, pray tell, is the name of this evil king?"

This time the reply came from the front of the RV, as Zach put the vehicle in gear and pulled away from the sidewalk. "Arthur Jamison."

He applied more pressure to the gas pedal and the RV started rolling up the street.

Cole frowned. "And why would you want to do this?"

Jeremy dropped the shotgun on the floor and kicked it away as he plopped into a recliner opposite the couch. This seemed an egregiously lackadaisical way of handling a potentially deadly weapon. It didn't discharge, however, and Cole chose to take this as an indication that it wasn't actually loaded. He sure hoped so, anyway, because that would suggest these guys might not be quite as crazy as they seemed right now.

"We've been trying to find Tyler," Jeremy told him. "Calling all around town, visiting his favorite places, but he has vanished. We grew concerned and began to take drastic steps."

Cole glanced around at the spacious interior of the RV. "I can see that. Maybe I'm misremembering, but I was under the impression the Subaru was the only working vehicle you guys had. So where did this monstrosity come from?"

The Ronald Reagan mask briefly turned toward them again as Zach said, "We commandeered it. Soon we wade into battle. A battle that will be fierce and fraught with peril. The Subaru has been a trusty vessel, but it would not be suitable to the glorious task at hand. We needed a *mighty battleship!*"

The way Zach's voice rose sharply on those last two words almost made Cole laugh, but he didn't because he knew he had to quickly dissuade these clowns from doing anything rash. He'd arrived at a tentative truce with Arthur Jamison and his daughter, and the last thing he needed was for these guys to ruin that by roping him into their shenanigans. They were only two blocks away from the old man's high-rise fortress, so time was short.

He took a big breath and let it out. "Let me explain why this isn't a good idea in terms you motherfuckers can understand. A frontal assault on the evil king's fortress cannot succeed because it's protected by an even more evil dark wizard using, uh, really, really dark and powerful magic, as well as by many, many trolls armed with boom-sticks. I can help you defeat the magic and the trolls, but first we must journey to the fabled kingdom of Antioch."

They were stopped at a traffic light now, the last one before they could proceed unimpeded to the high-rise. Zach and Jeremy looked at each other without saying a thing until after the light turned green. This didn't change until horns started honking behind them.

Zach started driving up the road while his head was still turned toward the rear part of the RV. "Why Antioch?"

Cole cringed, gripping the edges of the couch cushions to either side of him. "Man, watch the fucking road. And we need to go to Antioch to retrieve an enchanted object. With it, we can defeat the evil wizard's dark magic and kick massive amounts of ass. So I guess the question is, do you want to do this right, or do you want to do it the extra fucking dumb way?"

Zach brought the RV to a stop in the street outside the high-rise. He and Jeremy again spent some moments staring at each other without speaking. How they could read each other for non-verbal cues with their faces covered, Cole did not know. Perhaps they were communicating on a telepathic level. Maybe it had something to do with the substances they'd ingested. It was hard to tell.

Then they nodded.

Zach shifted around in his seat and faced the windshield. He goosed the gas pedal and the big RV started rolling up the street again. "Onward to Antioch."

THIRTY-FIVE

CONSIDERING HIS ALTERED STATE OF mind, Zach took them out of the downtown area and out to the interstate with a surprising minimum of fuss. He did take the wrong exit at the junction the first time, but was easily able to come back to the junction and take the correct one.

They were two miles out of the city before Cole decided he had to ask about this. "Dude, I can't get over how well you're driving."

Zach glanced back at him. "What do you mean?"

Cole laughed. "Last time I saw you fuckers, you were starting to trip, and I know that shit can't have worn off yet. I don't indulge, personally. Strictly a beer and weed guy. But from being around people I know who do psychedelics, driving is usually out of the question."

Jeremy said, "We took a mild-ish dose."

Zach added, "And we are experienced users."

Cole grunted.

It was basically what they'd told him back at their apartment much earlier in the evening.

They drove on in silence for about another half mile before something compelled Cole to blurt out. "You guys wouldn't believe what happened to me earlier. Pretty sure it was way freakier than any acid trip."

Zach glanced at him again. "Go on."

Cole told them about his consciousness briefly entering Katelyn's mind and assuming control of her body. Perhaps predictably, this required him to brush off a few crude questions regarding anatomy, but they voiced no skepticism regarding the truth of his account. He also told them what little he knew about the Time Keys and their possible connection to the incident. Again, no doubt was expressed.

"You know, most people would tell me I was crazy after hearing this shit."

Zach chuckled. "Most people don't see behind the veil the way we do. They go around with blinders on to protect themselves, to keep from seeing the madness and evil on which society itself is built."

Jeremy gave an emphatic nod, making the tall ears of his rabbit head flop about. "They don't want to see the truth about our so-called leaders. The lizard skin beneath the soft pink flesh."

Cole pursed his lips. "Hmm."

Zach said, "And Arthur Jamison is one of the worst. An ultimate predator disguised as a philanthropist. He's personally arranged at least a dozen political assassinations. Always manipulating world events behind the scenes with the rest of his uber-rich friends."

"And you know this how?"

Jeremy laughed. "*Everybody* knows. It's an open secret kind of thing. They get away with it by having all the right people dismiss it as conspiracy bullshit, sowing seeds of doubt and plausible deniability. Painting those awakened to the truth as crackpots. Sometimes conspiracy theories *are* bullshit, but not when it comes to this motherfucker. He's the real deal. A man behind the curtain, one of them anyway. Pulling strings, making the sheep dance."

They lapsed into silence for a few minutes after that. Cole mulled over all he'd been told. He was positive some of it—especially that hoary old lizard people crap—was sheer nonsense. Given much of what he'd seen and experienced tonight, however, some of it wasn't at all easy to write off as drug-fueled lunacy.

"Can I ask you guys something totally unrelated?"

Zach said, "Shoot."

There was an open carton of Budweiser on the table anchored to the floor in the middle of the living space. Cole helped himself to one, offering money that was turned down. He popped the can open and took a sip, sighing in relief at his first taste of beer since resolving— from his perspective—the Tyler situation.

"What's up with the masks?"

Dead silence for an uncomfortable period of time.

Zach and Jeremy began to squirm in their seats. Jeremy whined and began touching the front of his mask, squeezing the rubber nose and pulling at the long fake whiskers. Cole's head swiveled back and forth as he eyed each of them in turn multiple times, his face contorting in a way that reflected a deepening anxiety. His question had touched a nerve, it seemed, which confused the hell out of him, because it'd seemed fairly innocuous.

"You know what, guys? Forget I asked. Seriously."

Zach said, "It's just such a strange question. Why are you asking about masks?"

Jeremy nodded. "Yeah, dude. Halloween is months away."

Cole guzzled beer as he continued glancing back and forth between them. There was such earnestness in their voices. They seemed genuinely confused and weren't simply messing with him. This further deepened his own considerable level of anxiety.

He shook the beer can. It was empty already. He grabbed a fresh one from the carton and sat back down after first almost stumbling over his feet. His head felt swimmy in a way that made him realize the quest to track down Katelyn had not magically burned away all the alcohol in his system. His intake over the course of the evening had been prodigious, so that made sense. It was only just now catching back up to him, in the wake of so many stressful incidents.

He cracked open the new can and took another big gulp.

And then, perhaps because the strange tension of the moment was just too much to bear, he blurted out the thing that was still hovering at the forefront of his mind. "Goddammit. You are both wearing masks. Fucking ridiculous ones."

A silent beat elapsed.

Then Zach snorted and shook his head. "No, dude, we're not."

"But you are."

"But we're not."

Cole gulped beer. "Are, too."

"D2."

Jeremy abruptly stood and twisted his torso about, holding his arms weirdly in front of him as he did a half-assed impression of

Robbie the Robot. "Beep boop, does not compute."

He then dashed to the rear of the RV, pulled open a door, and slipped into what Cole figured was a bathroom, though he couldn't see inside it from where he sat. The door stood open as Jeremy remained inside for several seconds.

Then Jeremy started screaming.

Cole groaned.

Fuck.

He chugged down the remainder of his second can of Bud and immediately grabbed another one. In his opinion, it had become scientifically impossible to deal with even one more second of this madness without getting blind drunk. A basic level of frat boy drunkenness would not suffice. No, he needed to go beyond that, to journey to a realm of brain-frying intoxication so extreme it might not be possible to ever return.

Jeremy was still screaming as he came running out of the bathroom and started grabbing at the rabbit head and throwing himself about the interior of the RV. He crashed against both walls and bounced off the table many times. Once he fell across Cole's lap and rolled away, bouncing right back up as he continued to scream and tear at the rabbit head. It was by far the most absurd thing Cole had ever personally witnessed. The rabbit head looked like it would easily come flying off as a result of the histrionics if not for Jeremy clutching at it, yet he was acting as if it was permanently attached to his flesh.

A distraught-sounding Zach yelled at him. "Dude, calm down! What the fuck is wrong with you?"

Jeremy paused in his screaming long enough to say, "Fuck off, Ronald Reagan! I've turned into a bunny rabbit! We're all the way through the looking glass!"

He resumed screaming.

Zach had twisted around in the driver's seat and was staring at his friend. "Ronald Reagan?"

He started trying to touch his face and commenced to immediately freaking out when his fingers felt rubber instead of flesh. The one hand he still had on the steering wheel came away as he scrambled out of the driver's seat and went running toward the bathroom, knocking Jeremy over in the process.

Cole watched him disappear through the open door.

Then his head swiveled back toward the front of the RV.

"Oh, shit."

BURNING DOWN THE NIGHT

He dropped his beer and hurried to the front of the vehicle, jumping over Jeremy's sprawled form before sliding into the driver's seat. The vehicle was still in motion, of course, the speedometer needle hovering at right around 60 MPH. This was distressing enough, but the RV had already veered onto the shoulder of the interstate and was on a collision course with the guardrail.

Cole grabbed the steering wheel and pulled hard.

THIRTY-SIX

NEXT CAME A SOUND OF rending metal as the side of the RV scraped the guardrail. The big vehicle swayed and, for a dizzyingly terrifying moment, Cole feared it would go over the rail and tumble down the hill beyond it. He held tight to the wheel and continued pulling hard at it, gritting his teeth so hard it caused even more damage to them. The scraping and tearing sounds went on for a few more moments and they were soon accompanied by the loud pops of tires blowing out. His foot stayed on the brake, too, as he worked hard to bring the thing to a stop. Meanwhile, behind him, the clearly insane music shop clerks were still throwing themselves around and screaming. All of it came together in a way that made Cole feel like he was trapped inside the most demented carnival funhouse ride ever devised.

Miraculously, however, his desperate attempt to save them all seemed on the verge of succeeding. The speedometer needle continued a steep leftward trend, falling below 20 MPH. Then under 10 MPH. Then down to a crawl as, with a final sound of metal shredding, he was at last able to guide the RV away from the guardrail.

He brought the Winnebago to a full stop right at the edge of the highway. Heaving what felt like the biggest sigh of relief he'd ever breathed, he put the vehicle in park, removed the keys from the ignition, and slid out of the driver's seat.

The guys had stopped screaming by then. They were still wearing the stupid masks, but otherwise seemed back to normal. Relatively speaking. They said nothing as he brushed past them and snatched the carton of Bud up from the floor, where it must have fallen in the chaos.

"I'm taking your beer, assholes. It's the least of what you owe me after this."

Jeremy pulled at his rabbit whiskers. "Where are you going?"

"I don't fucking know, but I'm bailing on this clown show."

Zach said, "But what about the enchanted object? We still need it to defeat the evil king."

Cole went to the side door and tried to open it. The mangling the side of the vehicle had taken during its encounter with the guardrail made this more difficult than it normally would be. He started kicking at it and after a few times the door flew open.

He glanced back at them as he moved into the opening. "There is no enchanted object. That was a lie to keep you from doing something stupid. Let it go, guys. You're never gonna see Tyler again. Don't ask me how I know, but I fucking *know*, okay? Give it up. Your quest is over. Nobody gets a happy ending."

He stepped out of the vehicle and started walking up the shoulder of the road. Cars flashed by on the highway, the wind left in their wake stirring his hair. Inside them were people headed to Antioch and locations beyond. At this late hour, many were probably returning to their suburban homes after a night of partying in the city. A lot of potential DUI candidates. Some drivers honked to indicate annoyance at how close he was to the road. They had a point, he guessed. It was unnerving to have metal objects weighing well over a ton hurtling past him at high rates of speed, many passing within a few feet. His guts clenched every time another one blew past him. After surviving so much craziness, getting smeared all over the highway would be a lame-ass way to go. He stopped walking up the shoulder and approached the guardrail to study the terrain below. A street lamp a short distance from where he stood allowed him to realize he recognized this piece of land.

He was close to Antioch. The exit was probably only a few miles away. A few miles on foot on the shoulder of the road in broad daylight would have been doable. Not ideal, but doable. In the dark wee hours of the morning with a carton of beer tucked under his arm, though? Not so much. Sticking a thumb out for a ride probably also wasn't a great idea. No sane person would pick him up at this hour, but a serial killer might. There'd also be an excellent chance of attracting the attention of a cop. Getting arrested wouldn't be much fun, either.

There was just one thing he could do.

He swung a leg over the guardrail.

"Can we come with you?"

That was when he realized Zach and Jeremy had been silently following him the whole time. This felt mildly creepy at first, but the sheepish tone in Zach's voice made him feel sorry for them. They were still wearing the masks, but were calmer now.

Cole sighed. "We're gonna be walking down a fairly steep hill into a ravine. Be careful of your footing or you'll fall all the way down."

He swung his other leg over the guardrail and started making his way down the hill. Heeding his own advice, he exercised as much caution as he could given his state of inebriation. He worked to maintain his balance and be sure of his footing with each step down. This wasn't made any easier by the vegetation that became denser the farther down he went. He couldn't always see where his feet were landing and had to go by feel more often than not. At first, light from the street lamp above aided his progress, but by the time he was perhaps a third of the way down, encroaching darkness became more of a factor. There was a stand of trees further down and he would have to pass through them to get to where he was going. The darkness would be deeper inside the canopy of trees, of course, but once he was beyond them, moonlight should be sufficient to guide him the rest of the way.

Each time he glanced back to verify that Zach and Jeremy were still descending behind him, he was surprised all over again to see them continuing to proceed with the requisite amount of caution. Despite their silence during the descent, they still seemed calm and unperturbed by the challenge of making their way down the hill in the dark. It was such a stark contrast to their previous crazed behavior, and a radical shift he wouldn't have thought possible within so short a period of time. A part of him wanted to ask them about it, but he refrained, fearing that even broaching the subject of their bizarre freakout would set off another manic episode. That they were still wearing those stupid masks was unsettling enough.

They became more vocal once they were all inside the stand of trees, one of them making noises Cole needed a moment to recognize as an attempt to simulate static from a walkie-talkie. It was a pretty good attempt, too, almost eerily realistic in the deeper darkness. Pretty soon both of them were doing it with a nearly equal level of adeptness, as well as simulating distorted voices emerging from the imaginary walkie-talkies. Frequent references to "Charlie" and "clicks" soon clued him in that they were now pretending to be American soldiers out on patrol in wartime Vietnam.

Almost on level ground by that point, Cole decided it was now safe to pop open another beer. He dug a can out of the carton and popped the tab, taking a swig. His traveling companions reacted to the hiss of the can opening, one shouting at the other to take point and check the trees for signs of Charlie. There was a rustling sound as one ran forward and pressed his back against a tree. Then came more simulated walkie-talkie noises and a frantic attempt to call in an air strike. Simulated sounds of explosions and machine gun fire followed.

"I'm hit! Oh, Jesus. I'm hit."

"Medic! Medic!"

Cole chugged beer and kept walking.

Soon he emerged from the treeline and stood at the bank of the shallow creek. On the opposite side of the creek was another stand of trees. The other guys joined him there moments later, spreading out to stand to either side of him. Both had picked up sticks during their passage through the wooded area and were holding them like soldiers brandishing M-16s.

Zach said, "It's not safe out here in the open. We should take cover. There's VC everywhere."

"No can do, Private Joker." Cole pivoted and pointed in a leftward direction. "We're meeting up with another unit three clicks that way. Orders from on high. It's beaucoup important for strategic reasons. You'll just have to trust me. If we start taking fire, call in another air strike."

The guys glanced at each other and shrugged.

"Roger that," one of them said.

Cole drained the last dregs of beer, crushed the empty can, and tossed it into the creek. He wasn't a litterbug normally, but he was too drunk to care much by that point. He dug another can out of the carton and started walking up the rocky creek bank. Zach and Jeremy followed.

A period of relative silence ensued, during which the only sounds were the tread of their own feet and the gentle trickling of creek water. Then an owl started hooting somewhere out in the trees. One of the guys behind him started imitating the sound and the other soon followed suit. Once again, these were eerily accurate impressions, good enough for Cole to wonder if they'd ever considered getting into doing voice work in TV and film. He supposed it was possible they weren't even fully cognizant of the talent they possessed. Maybe they were only capable of it when they were high as fuck.

A little further up the creek bank, they slipped back into the Vietnam playacting scenario. This time it was less action-oriented. They talked about things they might do while on leave in Saigon, which mostly seemed to consist of getting drunk and fucking Vietnamese whores. They also discussed what they would do once they were finally able to rotate home, speaking wistfully of once again seeing their sweethearts and driving their old jalopies to the drive-in on a warm Saturday night. There was a lot of shifting between the war movies that were obviously influencing the scenario. Often they were vaguely referencing *Full Metal Jacket*, while at other times the source of inspiration was clearly either *Platoon* or *Apocalypse Now*.

The walk up the creek bank was taking far longer than Cole had anticipated, mostly due to the necessity of being extra sure of footing. There were many jagged rocks along the bank. A fall here would come with great risk of cracking his skull open. He drank three more beers before he heard the sound of a lighter flicking to life behind him. Then came a splash as something landed in the middle of the creek. Cole glanced backward and saw that Jeremy was no longer wearing the rabbit head. He had a fat joint pinched between his lips and was lighting it with a Zippo. As he was taking his first big draw off the joint, Zach tore off the Reagan mask and tossed it into the creek as well. They did this in so nonchalant a way that Cole couldn't help laughing.

The two of them passed the joint back and forth a few times before Zach offered it to Cole. "Want a hit?"

Cole shrugged. "Fuck it."

He took two big draws from the joint, holding each in his lungs for a prolonged moment before exhaling again. The second exhalation was followed by a brief coughing fit. After that, the joint was repeatedly passed between the three of them until it was down to a tiny nub. The quality of their weed was excellent, probably the best he'd ever had. He felt lighter of spirit than he had all night as they resumed walking up the bank. Reality itself was taking on a softer, dreamier aspect. It was nice, feeling disconnected like that. He could almost believe none of the terrible stuff he'd been through had actually happened, that it'd all just been some crazy dream.

At one point along the way, he veered back into the woods and returned with a stick of his own. The three of them then took up positions behind a particularly large slab of rock, intermittently peeking over it to fire their make-believe rifles at imaginary enemies. Cole got so into it he could almost see the blood flying as bullets perforated flesh and bodies fell. All of them dug more beers out of the rapidly emptying carton, the twenty-four cans it once held down to a couple. They continued to drink even as they emerged from cover and charged up the bank, firing their stick-rifles between swigs of beer.

Eventually Cole realized they were getting close to what he was now thinking of as the "rendezvous" point. He slowed their pace and started more carefully scanning the opposite side of the creek. Then he saw it, the big rock slab he'd slept on alone months ago. He studied the creek itself and judged it shallow enough to wade through to the other side.

After telling his companions what he had in mind, he stepped down to the edge of the water, hesitated, and glanced over at the opposite bank again. He gasped when he saw the slim, wispy figure standing atop the big rock. The man wore a ratty sweater and jeans with holes. Longish, dirty blond hair partially hid his face, but that didn't stop Cole from recognizing him. A chill went through him when the man looked down and met his gaze. He knew what he was seeing must be a hallucination induced by exhaustion and overindulgence. The guy was dead and probably in a morgue or funeral home on the other side of the country. He couldn't be standing on a creek bank in Tennessee. It simply wasn't possible. Knowing that didn't change the fact that, in that moment, the guy looked every bit as real and flesh and blood as anyone Cole had ever seen.

The dead rock star turned away from him and walked toward the stand of trees beyond the opposite bank, his apparent physical form wavering and then vanishing before even reaching the treeline. Like he'd never been there at all, which of course had to be the case.

Except . . .

"Did you guys see that?"

Zach and Jeremy were standing to either side of him again.

Zach sipped beer. "Something that looked like Kurt's ghost? Sure did."

Jeremy nodded. "Totally."

Zach said, "Except ghosts tend to be anchored to specific locations. To where they lived or died. Long distance spectral travel is rare."

"That was probably something else," Jeremy added. "Some spirit or entity that took a familiar form. One meaningful to all of us."

Cole frowned, disquieted by this notion. "But why? What does it mean?"

Zach shrugged. "This is only a semi-educated guess, but I think it means we should get the fuck on out of these spooky-ass woods as soon as goddamn possible."

Cole agreed.

In order to avoid taking a path that would directly intersect with where they'd last seen the entity—or whatever it was—they trudged a little farther along the edge of the creek before attempting to cross. Once they were on the other side, they approached the treeline warily, fearing an imminent reappearance of the entity. Cole's heart pistoned in overdrive as they again entered the woods and started making their way uphill. More than once he heard suspicious rustlings and low noises that felt like spirits whispering in his ear. Whispers that sounded like the voices of dead rock stars. Kurt, Jim Morrison, Elvis, John Lennon, Jimi, Janis, Sid Vicious, Johnny Thunders, Stiv Bators, Ian Curtis, and more. A chorus of ghostly sorrow. He was certain he felt a cold hand touch the side of his face.

He walked fast, breathing hard as they at last emerged from the stand of trees and stood on a hill where the rear ends of a row of apartment buildings faced the woods. Relief swept over him as his directional instincts were proven correct. He'd already sort of known it while down there on the opposite side of the creek, but it was wonderful to have visual proof. He felt bone-tired, like an ancient traveler through mystic lands at the end of a months-long journey. Like he could sleep for months. Tomorrow would be rough, with an epic hangover to endure and wounds to tend to, but at least he was here.

This was the complex in Antioch where his friends lived.

Some of Katelyn's words from earlier echoed in his mind, causing him to amend the thought.

His so-called friends lived here.

BURNING DOWN THE NIGHT

He waited for Zach and Jeremy to emerge from the woods, and when they did, they continued up the hill to the complex.

THIRTY-SEVEN

AT FIRST THERE WAS NO response as Cole banged a fist against the apartment's door. He heard no voices or music emanating from the other side, just dead silence. His fear was that everyone had cleared out in the wake of the violent intrusion. The only thing giving him any hope to the contrary was the presence of Spencer's turquoise Jeep Samurai down in the parking lot. It was entirely possible Spencer had departed in someone else's vehicle, but Cole continued pounding on the door anyway. He had no burning desire to see his so-called friends again, but he did need his keys, which should still be on the kitchen counter in the apartment.

A door to a unit at the front of the building opened and a man in boxer shorts stepped out onto the landing. "Yo, what's all the fucking noise about? Knock that shit off or I'm calling the cops. People are trying to sleep."

Zach popped the tab on the final can from the now empty beer carton. He sipped from it and said, "Here's something to consider. Cows are regarded as sacred or near sacred in some cultures, but in my opinion, they are evil creatures. Sheer, unadulterated evil. This is why we eat them. To curb the bovine menace. Think about that and know that the next time you have a Big Mac you are truly doing the

Lord's work."

The man stared blankly at him a moment before backing into his apartment, closing the door, and locking it.

Throughout this interaction, Cole's focus remained on the door in front of him as he continued to pound his fist against it. He was close to giving up when he at last heard someone approaching from the other side. There was a pause, during which Cole assumed someone was peering out at them through the peephole. Then he heard the sound of a deadbolt retracting and the door came open.

Spencer squinted at him through red-rimmed eyes. "Jesus, dude. What happened to your face?"

Cole grunted. "What do you think happened? I got the shit beat out of me. We're coming in."

He shouldered his way in without waiting for permission. There was some mumbling behind him as he headed straight for the kitchen, where he found his keys right where he'd left them. His remaining Heinekens were still in the fridge. There were fewer than he remembered, but that wasn't surprising. He snagged a bottle and popped the cap with a magnetic opener he grabbed off the fridge door.

Back in the living room, Spencer was looking askance at Zach and Jeremy. He hooked a thumb in their direction when he saw Cole emerge from the kitchen. "Who the fuck are these guys?"

Zach belched and said, "We are professional weirdos. When the going gets weird, we get weirder. I suddenly want to hear Slayer. Do you have any Slayer tapes?"

Cole said, "They work at Sound Stack."

Zach nodded. "That, too. Or maybe not. Due to an unfortunate incident, we may be forced to tender our resignations."

Spencer sighed and rubbed tiredly at his bleary eyes. "Whatever. I'm too out of it to care. And I'm not really into thrash metal, so I don't have any fucking Slayer tapes. Sorry." He looked at Cole. "Dude, I am so happy to see you again. I honestly thought I never would." He sniffled and had tears in his eyes as he said this. "I'm sorry I called that bitch. I fucked up. You've gotta believe me, I never would've if I'd had any idea."

Cole looked at the bottle in his hand after taking a sip from it. He knew from the first taste he wouldn't be finishing this one. Not because he was suddenly changing his ways. That wasn't ever going to happen. He was at his absolute limit and the beer tasted sour sliding down his gullet. The long bender was coming to an end.

He sighed. "Whatever, man. I don't feel like getting into it right now. It's been a long fucking night and I am beyond wiped. I'd head home right now, but I don't think I'm in any shape to drive."

Spencer started nodding along as he spoke. "Don't even worry about it, dude. You and your friends can crash here. I'm wiped, too. I was practically in a coma when I finally heard the racket you were making. So I'm gonna crash again, too. We'll talk shit out later. Okay, man?"

Cole ignored him and took a pointed look around. "Where'd everybody else go?"

Spencer was already headed toward the hallway. He spoke with his back turned to them. "Gone. Took the fuck off as soon as the coast was clear. More shit we can talk about tomorrow."

He disappeared from view and a moment later they heard the door to his room close at the end of the hallway. After a few last words with Zach and Jeremy—who assured him they'd be fine crashing in the living room—Cole wandered down the hallway and into the other bedroom. There was a digital radio alarm clock on the nightstand. It was a model he hadn't used before. He spent some time fiddling with it until he figured out how to use it, setting it to go off at eleven. With that taken care of, he kicked off his shoes, stretched out on the bed, and closed his eyes.

The next thing he knew, he was squinting against bright sunlight streaming in through the open slats of the window blinds. His head was throbbing and the inside of his mouth felt like it was lined with sandpaper. He groaned as he lifted his torso up slightly and turned his head to look at the alarm clock.

The numbers on the display read 11:47.

"Shit!"

He sat bolt upright and swung his legs over the side of the bed. A despairing moan escaped his lips as he stared at the numbers and tried to make sense of them. The sudden movement intensified the already severe ache in his head, but he didn't care. All that mattered was the calamity in progress, one that had befallen him as a consequence of his drunkenness. This was confirmed when he pressed a button on the device and saw that the alarm was activated, but it was set to go off at eleven at night instead of in the morning. It was the dumbest of all possible mistakes, one he never would have made while sober.

Memories of that sidewalk meeting with Katelyn came to vivid life in his head. *Noon on the dot.* That's what she'd said. They were going to take off together, get out of this nowhere place and never look back, but now the opportunity was slipping away. It might already be gone. She'd been so specific about the time to meet. Was there any chance in hell she'd wait for him?

Only one way to find out.

He stepped into his shoes, lacing them up fast and sloppy. They were loose on his feet as he grabbed his keys from the nightstand and ran out of the bedroom. Zach and Jeremy were passed out in the living room as he came racing through it, one oblivious on the couch while the other slept face-down on the floor. The TV was on with the sound muted, tuned to an episode of *Kids in the Hall*.

Outside the apartment, Cole pounded down the stairs to the sidewalk. He spied his Tercel and raced toward it, sliding in behind the wheel seconds later. There was live-wire agitation in all his movements by then, his whole body shaking as he started the car, backed out of the parking space, changed gears again, and started tearing his way through the complex at a reckless speed.

The recklessness continued once he was back out on the main road. He floored the gas pedal and started weaving in between and around other vehicles. The upright needle on the speedometer was like a figurative middle finger to the posted low speed limit. The whole time, he was aware he was at extreme risk of triggering police pursuit, but that didn't sway him. Nothing short of a spectacular crash on the highway would. The possibility of a glorious future awaited him somewhere out there. A chance at a better life. A life in which he was an actual participant instead of a spectator. One that would only be possible in the company of one special person. Someone to make him feel like anything was possible.

He made it to the highway without incident and floored the gas again, rocketing toward the city at over 90 MPH, once again weaving his way through a sea of vehicles cruising at somewhere just above the 55 MPH limit. Horns honked and cars veered away from him to avoid collisions. The blare of a police siren seemed imminent, like it should happen at any moment, but it never did. This felt a bit like the hand of fate itself clearing the way for him, but not necessarily in a benevolent way, more with a sense of malign glee and anticipation. He kept eyeing the clock, willing the minutes to pass slower, but the effort was futile. The minutes kept passing, falling faster and faster into the past as he entered the city and was forced to slow down and stop a seeming infinity of times as he made his way over to the downtown Greyhound station.

By the time he arrived and left the Tercel illegally parked at the curb outside the station entrance, it was nearly twenty minutes past noon. He was panting and sweating profusely as he ran into the station and took a look around, his eyes futilely trying to go everywhere at once. There was no sign of Katelyn at the ticket counter or in any of the seats in the waiting area. He walked all the way through the station to the doors in back, stepping outside to see passengers with bags in hand, waiting to board soon to depart buses. There was a thick stench of diesel fuel in the air. Multiple sets of eyes turned his way as he scanned the lines of people, and again saw no sign of her anywhere.

Noting that some of the buses had people in seats already, he approached each of them and tried studying the faces on the other side of the windows. He saw no one who even faintly resembled Katelyn.

His feeling of despair deepening, he reentered the station and took another look around, a slower and less frantic one. Again, there was no sign of her. He went up to the counter and inquired with the ticket agents, who didn't seem interested in helping him. His description of Katelyn was met with shrugs and looks of boredom. No one remembered seeing a girl who matched the description he gave.

Running out of options, he resorted to interrogating people in the waiting area. This was the surest sign of the desperation consuming him, because going up to a bunch of strangers in a setting like this was something he'd ordinarily never do. He didn't enjoy interacting with strangers in any setting, much less in a dour bus station filled with people who'd clearly rather be anywhere else. Most responded with shrugs and silent shakes of their heads. A few got angry and told him to leave them alone. One, an old man with a cane, threatened him with physical harm if he didn't shut up and move away from him.

At last, he surrendered to the inevitable.

To the undeniable.

She wasn't here. He hadn't missed her. She'd never been here in the first place. Not today, anyway.

Cole staggered over to the nearest row of seats and plopped into an open one at the end. He leaned back in the chair and felt all the energy drain from his body as he stared at the entrance. A faint hope still lived in his heart, but it was fading fast. Maybe she was running late. Maybe there'd been complications with Arthur Jamison. Maybe the old man wanted to squeeze a little more juice out of her before finally letting her go. Put her in one more dirty movie. Sell her to another gross old rich fucker for a night. There was no limit to the kind of sick and devious shit powerful men could get away with.

The explanation could be almost anything. Most of all he just wanted to believe she hadn't lied to him. That she hadn't been playing some cruel trick on him and really had wanted to run off somewhere with him. He felt stupid for a lot of the time he spent sitting in the station. Stupid and gullible. Who else would be so dumb to put so much trust into someone they barely knew? If this was happening against her will . . . well, that would be terrible, but at least it wouldn't be a betrayal.

After more than thirty minutes of sitting there and praying for her to miraculously materialize, he got up and staggered over to a change machine. He fed a bill into the slot, scooped the coins out of the tray, and made his way over to a pay phone near the entrance to the men's bathroom. He put the receiver to his ear, dropped a quarter in the slot, and punched in Arthur Jamison's number. A recording informed him the number had been disconnected.

He laughed and put the receiver back on the hook.

A ticket clipped under one of his wiper blades was waiting for him when he walked out of the bus station. He ripped it away, crumpled it into a ball, and tossed it over his shoulder before getting back inside the Tercel and driving away. His journey away from the station happened in a far more sedate manner than the approach. He felt numb as he steered his way through a random series of city streets. The aching sadness he knew he should be feeling wasn't there because he accepted this for what it was, for what it really meant. This was just the way things always worked out for people like him. The nobodies and the also-rans. The ugly and the unloved. There wasn't anything self-pitying in this. It was simply a sober recognition of how things really were.

He left the city and drove home.

A year went by.

He spent most of that time holed up in his bedroom, emerging only on occasion to buy beer. There were many frustrating discussions with his parents. Frustrating for them, that is. They were worried about him and urged him to seek help. Life was passing him by, they said. He was wasting what was left of his younger years by sinking into an emotional black hole. Cole told them he was no longer interested in saving himself and if they wanted to kick him out of their house, he would understand. Tears were shed, but that didn't happen. Spencer dropped by on occasion and made attempts to cajole him out of his seemingly terminal state of depression. It never worked. Zach and Jeremy made similar efforts that more often than not involved feeding him drugs.

That didn't work either.

Then one day a custom-made photo postcard addressed to him arrived in the mail. It showed a girl in a black dress with her back to the camera standing in front of a gaudy-looking house. She had short dark hair. There was no return address, but a house number was visible in the photo and the postmark stamp was from New Orleans.

On the back someone had written,

I'm free. Really free.

Come find me.

-K

The implications were obvious. He was meant to think this message was from Katelyn, and the girl in the photo certainly resembled her, but without seeing her face, it was impossible to be sure.

Maybe it really was from her. He desperately wanted to believe that, but he was much more cynical now and knew it might also be from someone wishing to lure him to a place somewhere far from home. Someone like Nikki, if she'd survived. Or Cindy. Or her father. Someone who might still want to hurt him, even after all this time.

But why wait so long to set the bait for such a trap?

By now any of those people had to know he was no threat at all.

And if it truly was from Katelyn, how would she have obtained his address?

Cole realized he could spend an eternity internally debating the matter from a hundred different angles and none of it would solve a thing. Only one thing might. The day after receiving the postcard, he boxed up most of his best remaining tapes, movies, and compact discs, holding back just a special few. He took the boxes to Zach and Jeremy at their new shop, where they gave him more than fair value.

Then he gassed up his car and drove away from his hometown.

Into the unknown.

Never to return.

Bryan Smith is the author of numerous novels and novellas, including *68 Kill, The Unseen, Slowly We Rot, Depraved,* and *Kill for Satan!,* which won a Splatterpunk Award for best horror novella of 2018. He won a second Splatterpunk Award in 2020 for *Dirty Rotten Hippies and Other Stories.* He is also the co-author of *Suburban Gothic,* written with Brian Keene. A film version of *68 Kill* was released in 2017. He lives in Tennessee with his dog Mac.

Check out the *Burning Down the Night* playlist:
https://open.spotify.com/playlist/1FSQWXZeGA0dizWCGHt8G
W?si=bb21944f54e84315

Other Grindhouse Press Titles